# Sterling Lakes Series, Book 4: Glory of the Heart

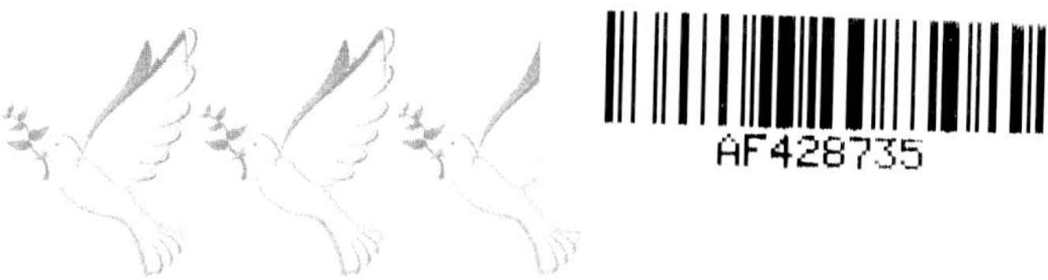

*A Contemporary Romance Series*
*Revised and Reissued*

## By Regina Andrews

Writers Exchange E-Publishing
http://www.writers-exchange.com

# Contents

# Dedication

With thanks to my husband Jon and all my family for their encouragement, love, and support. My thanks to Nicole Cunningham for her initial preparation of this manuscript and to Karen Wiesner for editing expertise. My heartfelt appreciation and thanks to Sandy Cummins, my wonderful publisher and editor, for her outstanding editorial direction and expertise in preparation of this manuscript, and especially for welcoming me so warmly to the Writers Exchange publishing family. Thank you, Sandy!

# *Chapter 1*

When she heard the steady pounding again, CC Cogshell realized it wasn't the bass beat of the Christmas music blaring in her earphones. She pulled them off, leaving them looped around her neck, to hear someone knocking on her front door.

"Be right there," she called, dusting her hands on her favorite holiday apron, albeit her most stained one. She contemplated taking it off for a moment before dismissing the idea as impractical, since she wasn't done working. Impatiently, she brushed her disarrayed ponytail of blond curls away from her face the way she had for the last several hours of nose-to-the-grindstone cookie-making.

*Who could be visiting her?* she wondered, still humming "Winter Wonderland" as she moved out of the open kitchen. She wasn't expecting anyone. Since moving into her cozy house in Sterling Lakes a few months earlier, she'd hardly had time to get to know anyone in town.

*Yet another visitor looking for Patty O'Malley's?* The Sterling Lakes Bed & Breakfast was just around the bend and a bit further down the pine-laden road from CC's cottage.

"We have company, Bella." On her way past, she gently rubbed the head of her elderly black and white cat, reclining lazily on a bar stool at the counter. "Mind that icing for me, will you, old lady? You know it's for the cookies later on so don't even think about it."

Bella had left behind the days when she would jump on the counter and CC would return to find her licking away at the icing as if dinner was served. Now, the feline glared in scorn at her accusation, nonchalantly groomed her paw as if anything else was beneath her.

"I still remember the face full of frosting I used to come back to, Little Miss, so don't give me that look."

Bella stood and turned her back to her with a look of pure disdain that had CC laughing her way to the front door.

Once there, she peered through the sheer curtain on the sidelite window to see who was outside. In the fairytale snowfall beyond stood someone tall with a broad back wearing a sheepskin jacket and a knit hat.

Frowning, she squinted around the drive in front of the house for a vehicle, but she didn't see one. Her cell phone rang, and she pulled back quickly to retrieve it from the pocket of her apron. Caller IDed Patty O'Malley.

"You busy, CC?" the older woman asked when she answered.

"Still making the cookies for the potluck supper. And getting the door. There's a strange guy outside."

"Well, you're the detective. Who is he?"

"I'm technically not a detective anymore. And I don't have a clue!"

"Are you getting repairs done on the house?"

"Nope."

"Is he cute?"

The teasing note in Patty's voice made her smile and shake her head while she peeked out the curtain again. "Hard to tell. Looks like he might have nice shoulders," she reported.

"Maybe he's your Christmas present, showing up a little early."

"I just turned twenty-six. I'm single, and I'm loving it."

Patty's hearty laugh rang out so CC had to pull the phone away from her ear, wincing. "Methinks thou dost protest too much. See you later at the potluck. I'll be getting to the church in a little while."

"Okay. Talk to you later." After hanging up, CC slipped her phone back into her pocket. The man still stood on the front steps, but he'd turned to face the door now. His breath made steam vapor clouds against the crimson December twilight.

When he leaned forward to ring the doorbell, she opened the door, offering a small smile. "Hi. Sorry I took so long. In the middle of something. Can I help you?" She sounded friendly, and he responded in kind.

"Hello. No problem. I'm intruding." He removed his hat and slipped it into his jacket pocket.

CC caught her breath. Snowflakes danced and swirled around him, settling on his dark hair and longer-than-legal eyelashes. He seemed about her age. *Okay, Patty wasn't wrong. This guy's the walking definition of gorgeous. If he can't be in my Christmas stocking, showing up at my front door is the next best thing.*

With his smoldering eyes dancing with energy and intelligence, the strong lines of his clean-shaven face, and an aristocratic nose, he made her think of a classic knight in shining armor from fairytale reading days.

"Are you looking for Patty O'Malley's?" she managed to ask, mentally kicking herself for letting her voice sound so breathless.

His chocolate brown eyes seemed strangely sentimental. He shook his head. "Actually, I've found what I'm looking for right here."

"What are you looking for?"

*Do I know him somehow and just don't recognize him?*

She was almost certain she couldn't have forgotten that face. "Do we know each other?" she asked without waiting for him to answer her first question.

"No, we haven't met yet. I'm Perrin Stafford."

When he offered her his hand, she instinctively reached to accept it. His hand was large and rough, but she found it more than a little pleasant against her much smaller, softer one. "Cydney Cogshell-- CC to my friends."

Movement at her feet startled her, and then Bella was scooting out the door and racing headlong into the front yard. Not only was she defying her age but also her usual unwillingness to get anywhere near the cold white stuff.

"Oh no--Bella! What are you doing, old lady?"

"I'll get her," Perrin said, darting after the tracks her cat had left in the snow.

Moving out to the porch without her jacket, CC watched with her arms crossed, shivering. Perrin crossed the snow-covered ground toward the huge oak tree where Bella had scampered. As if baiting him, Bella lifted one paw in the air.

"Careful, she's skittish," CC called to Perrin once he'd closed in on the feline. She didn't want to bother the Sterling Lakes Fire Department tonight with a 'cat up a tree' call.

In one smooth motion, Perrin scooped Bella up in his arms and strolled back to the front stoop. Unpredictably, Bella snuggled up against his chest, just as warm and cozy as could be. "This one has a mind of her own," he commented with a grin once he reached the porch.

"That she does. It's part of what I love about her."

"You call her 'old lady'?"

CC laughed. "It's a long story. I call her that affectionately, I assure you."

"I love it," he said, chuckling.

Their hands brushed in the exchange when he handed Bella over. He noticed how cold she was while she noticed the exact opposite. They laughed again, and she said, "Thanks for getting her. She must be getting senile in her old age. I don't know what that was about."

From inside the house, she heard something that'd been going on in the back of her mind for the last few minutes. She recognized it then as the oven timer. "My cookies! Come in!"

She rushed inside to save the last two batches, leaving him to follow at her thrown-over-her-shoulder invitation. She set Bella back on her favorite stool and grabbed two potholders.

Only when both pans of cookies were out did she breathe a sigh of relief. "Saved 'em!" she said when she turned back to see him standing at the edge of the kitchen. "So, are you a neighbor? I just moved to Sterling Lakes. I only know Patty O'Malley and a few others in town so far."

"Honestly, I used to live in this house when I was growing up. I haven't been back to Sterling Lakes in a long time, but I'm passing through now. I had a crazy impulse to see the old homestead again for old times' sake."

His gaze roamed lovingly across dark wood beam floors and up newly painted walls to crown molding on the high Victorian ceiling in the entryway. "Lots of good memories. Like I never left."

"A house can do that, especially if you were happy here."

He seemed sincere, but the former detective in her never took anything for granted. Try as she might, she couldn't remember any owners named 'Stafford' when she'd been researching the house, intending to buy.

"I've only lived here for a few months." She glanced at her watch. "The thing is, I'm making these cookies for a potluck at the church and I really need to get going..."

"I get it. Thanks anyway. I knew it was a long shot when I had the impulse. But I'll be in town for a couple days. Any chance...?"

"Where are you staying?"

He told her Patty's, and she said, "Okay. Well, we'll see."

Smiling, he nodded, accepting her vague response and the offer of one of the cookies she'd frosted earlier. After slipping his hat back on, he said goodbye, adding, "I can see myself out. I know you have to get the rest of these cookies frosted. Thanks for this one."

"Nice to meet you," she called when she could get hold of herself for all the questions bombarding her mind. She found herself following him, but he was already out the front door.

Snow swirled in the porch light outside and starlight twinkled against the glistening snow beyond. CC saw a solitary figure in what could have been a snow globe, hunched against the cold, clearly munching on her cookie.

When she turned, telling herself she had to get going and didn't have time to primp her appearance first, she found Bella standing in her path, giving her a reproachful look.

"You're acting very strange, old lady," CC told her warmly, shaking her head. "What in the world has gotten into you?"

Transformed into a winter wonderland, with decorated fir trees and artificial snow, the basement of St. Luke's Church bustled with activity for the annual pre-Christmas potluck supper.

"There you are!" Patty O'Malley greeted CC the minute she walked in, taking the bags of frosted cookies from her so she could shake the snow off her coat and scarf.

CC did a double-take, noticing Patty's sparkling eyes and flushed cheeks. "You look great, Patty."

"Thanks."

"But there's something different about you."

Patty shrugged innocently. "Not really."

"Anything going on? Is it you and Elwood?"

Patty nodded. "He's the man of my dreams! Details later. Too many eyes and ears here now." Her tone was conspiratorial.

Elwood Stewart was one of the wealthiest widowers in the area. Patty had hinted to CC a few times that they'd hit it off over the summer.

CC looked around the kitchen crowded with Women's Guild workers and volunteers. Definitely not a place for divulging something interesting that could have the whole town talking the next day.

"Let's set these cookies up on the dessert table."

"Sure thing." CC took the decorative plates Patty handed her while she carried the cookies over to the dessert table set up against the far wall.

Someone tapped her shoulder in the crossing. Turning, CC saw Millie Humboldt in her signature gingham dress and beehive hairdo. As head of the St. Luke's Women's League, she was feared by all as far as CC could tell from her few short months of attending Mass at the church. Fascinated by the woman's frozen smile, she almost missed what she was saying. "Hi, Millie. What was that? Sorry but I couldn't hear you."

"I said I was glad you could make it tonight, CC. Did you make those cookies or buy them?"

"Homemade. Baking is one of my hobbies."

"Really? I wouldn't think a Boston detective would have much time for hobbies."

"I'm not a detective anymore. But I guess it's like anything--if you're interested in something, you'll make time," CC answered as good-naturedly as she could. "Have a good time tonight!"

Moving past her, she joined Patty and began arranging cookies. This hadn't been the first uncomfortable exchange she'd had with

Millie since moving to town. Apparently, lots of folks in the parish had experienced run-ins with Millie and her nosiness.

"Elwood proposed to me," Patty whispered since they had a moment where no one was nearby.

Clearly, she'd been about to burst with this news, and CC hugged her, saying, "I knew something was different. I'm thrilled for you."

"I'm thrilled for me!"

CC laughed.

Once they finished putting out the cookies, Patty glanced behind her. "Hey, look who just walked in."

CC pivoted to see who had caught the other woman's attention. "That's the guy who was at my house!" she whispered urgently.

In surprise, CC watched him move through the crowd in the auditorium. Men shook his hand, women embraced him, and children danced gleefully at his feet.

*He's more popular than Santa Claus.*

"Perrin Stafford was at your house?" Patty asked.

"That's why I was late. Do you know him? I mean, beyond that he's staying at your B&B?"

"The guy's a national hero."

"What do you mean?"

"He's a war veteran, CC. He served in Afghanistan and was decorated for bravery."

"Well, now I feel like a heel for not trusting him."

Patty laughed, waving her hand dismissively. "Don't worry about it. You didn't know him from Adam. I'm sure he understood. Besides, I've heard...well, let's just say, he gets around with the ladies. Look at him. That's not hard to believe, given how gorgeous he is and coming from California. But that's just a rumor."

"Sounds scandalous." CC couldn't help shaking her head benevolently. "But I don't pay attention to rumors, Patty. If I did, I'd make sure I always had a camera and a gun at hand when I'm on the phone since, supposedly, detectives get distracted while talking on the phone and that's when the bad guys trip us up."

Perrin looked up from his conversation across the room, and his gaze met hers. She smiled, and his expression warmed. A moment later, he was moving toward her. CC couldn't seem to take her eyes off him. His whole persona, from his tall, muscular physique to his personality seemed to radiate a relaxed approachability she found irresistible.

"What's he back in town for anyway?" CC asked quickly, glad that at least she was capable of speaking out loud instead of standing, paralyzed, waiting for Perrin to arrive.

"He's working on the renovations of St. Luke's Church." As soon as she told her, Patty scampered away.

CC felt her cheeks turning bright red for no reason whatsoever. Feeling silly, she said quickly when Perrin was standing in front of her, "Imagine seeing you here."

"I wasn't actually planning it, though it probably looks like I was."

He moved past her to the dessert table and plucked up another of her frosted sugar cookies. "These are delicious. I've been craving another since I had the first."

"Good. We probably won't run out anytime soon. I made enough to feed an army."

Letting her glance linger on him, she waited for what he might say next, but he didn't seem to be in any particular rush to keep talking...although he enjoyed the second cookie thoroughly while he stayed mute. "So...you weren't planning to come here?" she asked him.

"No. I wanted to take a walk and you mentioned St. Luke's. I went to church here with my family when I was a kid. The rest of it was serendipity."

CC glanced over at him, frowning with a small smile of uncertainty. "Serendipity? How so?"

He polished off the cookie, then looked down at her. "Because I was hoping I'd see you again."

# *Chapter 2*

Perrin viewed the cozy scene in the church hall and felt nostalgia tugging at his heart, despite his misgivings coming to Sterling Lakes at all. Some of the sophisticated people he knew in California, with its unbridled opulence, would sniff at the handmade decorations in the humble basement.

"Welcome back to you, Major Stafford." Millie Humboldt smiled up at him.

"Thank you, ma'am," he answered politely.

His gaze never left CC for long. She was still by the dessert table, looking sweet with her attractively disheveled hair and big, cornflower blue eyes. She wore little makeup--and didn't need it. She had natural beauty he'd noticed from the moment she opened her front door to him. At that time, she'd had powdered sugar all over her face, and he'd found it utterly adorable, in part because she'd seemed so unaware of the situation.

*What a contrast to the women I know in California, who probably go to bed with full makeup on and are always "ready", even on days off. I've almost forgotten there are females in the world who aren't so aware of their own appearances and attracting guys and they're just themselves. Always.*

*The way Diane was...*

Coming back to Sterling Lakes this Christmas-time showed him that nothing much had changed here. But he had. His heart had been broken, his dreams shattered, his vows...vanished. But that didn't alter the good, solid start he'd gotten in Sterling Lakes. His strength and fortitude learned here allowed him to meet the challenges he'd faced in life, though even those had come to an end when he lost what mattered most to him.

He took in the decorated trees in the church hall, with its tiled floor and wood- paneled walls. Inhaling deeply, he appreciated the scent of fresh evergreen wreaths--no doubt a craft project of the women's church group.

The sentimentality turned his thoughts to his late wife, Diane. She would have loved this, and she knew how much this town meant to him. She would have respected all his connections. Coming from a small timber town in Canada, she'd understood the importance of such a close knit community, centered around God, just the way Sterling Lakes was.

Impulsive anger reminded him of the reason he almost hadn't come back here: God had taken Diane from him two agonizing years earlier, taken her from a world where she was doing so much good as an advocate for the homeless.

Shaking himself out of his dark thoughts took effort, and he asked himself yet again why he'd accepted Cascade Preston's invitation to work on the renovations of St. Luke's Church. A renowned stained glass artist from town, she'd also grown up in Sterling Lakes. He and Cascade had stayed in touch for a long time after he'd left town. She knew about his tours of duty in Afghanistan as well as his reputation as a marble sculptor.

Cascade had never met Diane, though maybe she knew he'd been married and lost his wife. At the very least, Perrin thought the fact that they'd never talked about it was a good thing. He didn't need anyone else telling him to just get over it, that Diane wouldn't want him moping around, avoiding life instead of living it in her absence. *Sometimes I believe I don't really want to move on, ever. That it's more comfortable for me to hang on to the memories, stay shrouded where I don't have to face reality. Alone.*

One of his commanding officers used to say all the time, "A brave heart never stays in the shadows." He hadn't been talking only about the losses everyone who participated in war experienced-- horrible tragedies like soldiers dying in the line of duty, leaving behind grieving widows and children who might not be able to define exactly what they were missing but the hole would always be there. In some ways, that kind of valor meant something. There was a reason, a justification for such tragedy. But Perrin had never felt that way about his wife's death. There'd been no valor, no romance, no glory in the fight. He and Diane had fought hard. They'd lost anyway. One day, she was no longer there, just gone, a victim of a horrible, debilitating and seemingly arbitrary disease that robbed him of the person he'd planned to share his life with.

*Over in a minute. But it doesn't feel over. It doesn't feel like it'll ever be over for me, and letting it be over...wouldn't that be another unfair travesty in the war with cancer?*

Why had he come here? The answer that came to him instantly bothered him almost more than anything else had for the past couple years: To get on with his life. Somehow.

CC was about to take a drink of punch just as Perrin said, "Patty looks happy. More than usual."

"Elwood Stewart, one of the most eligible rich widowers in the area, just proposed to her."

Lifting his paper cup, Perrin said, "A toast then: To a new beginning."

"To a new beginning."

They raised their cups, touching the rims mid-air, then both drank to the sentiment.

After her sip, she said, "So I hear you're a marble sculptor. That's unusual. How'd you get your start, considering you were also a soldier?"

"My dad. He worked in the granite quarry in the next town, Clarke's Falls, when I lived here as a kid."

"Interesting."

He nodded. "How long have you lived here?"

"Not even six months."

"You moved from where?"

"Back Bay."

"Oh, Boston." His eyes crinkled with a smile. "So you're a city girl."

CC laughed because she'd thought of that contrast so much since her move. "I guess. I never considered myself one."

"Miss Independent then?"

"That's the kind of thing I usually say when I'm trying to be cool and coy, but you beat me to it."

He chuckled. "So do you still work in Boston and commute?"

"I do. I used to be a detective with the Boston police, but I transferred to another department at the precinct about six months ago. I was a desk detective type. I did a lot of research. And now I still spend most of my time at a desk."

"No car chases?" he teased.

"Nope. I do translations. I transferred to the Interrogations and Intelligence Translation. It suits me so much better."

"What languages?"

"The romantic ones: Italian, French."

"I'm intrigued. You're in an unusual profession, too. We have something in common."

"And you're a war hero and legend here in Sterling Lakes. Everyone's excited that you're back."

"I didn't actually plan to come here. Cascade Preston got me involved in the church renovations. When she heard they wanted to re-do the altar and baptismal font, she called me. Cascade grew up in Sterling Lakes. Everyone knew my father, the mason, when I was growing up here. His work in stone and granite ensured he got a lot of contracts and worked all over this area, even in some churches."

"It sounds like a tremendous amount of work. How long do you expect the work to take you?"

Perrin shrugged. "Hard to tell, there are so many variables. But, once I have everything I need, the work shouldn't take more than a few weeks at the most."

"Wow, I assumed years."

"Most people do, but once I'm in the zone, it doesn't take long to bring my vision to life."

"Then you'll head back to California?" she guessed.

"Probably," he answered vaguely. "Looks like Father Greene's about ready to say grace. Should we sit down?"

"Sure." CC was surprised at the abrupt change in his tone. *His California life is obviously off limits, not to be discussed.*

When they sat next to Patty and Elwood, Perrin congratulated them, and Patty said good-naturedly, "So much for keeping that under wraps."

They all laughed, then Patty asked Perrin, "How are you liking our little potluck supper? Not like the glitz of California, I imagine?"

Perrin lifted an eyebrow. "California seems very far away to me at the moment. Sterling Lakes will always be home to me, I guess."

"Maybe it's the hand of God," Patty suggested.

Perrin offered a put-on-the-spot laugh. "I'm not sure I'm ready for that."

CC couldn't help wondering what would prompt him to say something like that.

Father Greene held up his hands and a hush fell over the animated church hall. The parishioners all joined hands together, uniting everyone in the hall, many with bowed heads.

"Thank you all for being here at our humble potluck dinner this evening," Father Greene said, "and for supporting our beloved St. Luke's renovation efforts. We welcome back our brother, Perrin

Stafford, and pray for his happiness and safety. Bless him for his service to our country and to our parish. We also celebrate with Patty O'Malley and Elwood Steward, who just this night announced their engagement."

Under her breath, Patty whispered, "*Announced* isn't exactly the case. How...? Who...?"

"Not me!" CC whispered. But she had shared the news with Perrin, in private. He'd been with her since then so she knew he hadn't spread the news.

Father Greene continued unabated, "We wish them a future of joy blessed in God's love."

CC lifted her head and saw Perrin looking at her in a strange sort of wonder. She had no idea what it meant, but she couldn't help giving him a big smile which he returned.

# *Chapter 3*

"Tell me, Ms. CC, will I be seeing you at choir tomorrow morning? I keep waiting for you sing with us."

CC looked over her shoulder in the buffet line to find JB Norwood, head of the St. Luke's Vacation Bible School and choir director, eyeing her hopefully. His holiday sweater vest, trimmed in bright red and green plaid, gave him a natty air.

"Not sure about tomorrow, JB," she replied with a pleasant smile.

"You're a wonderful singer. Should you let that go to waste? Why not use it in God's service?"

CC blinked at him in surprise. "You heard me one night at Patty's sing-along right after I moved in. One night!"

"It's all I needed to know God has gifted you."

*Translation: The choir had been dwindling for years and they needed bodies and new blood.* She smiled, shaking her head 'no'.

"Our Christmas program is coming up very soon. I'll be frank: We need help. What can I do to convince you? I'm just asking that you join temporarily--for the holiday concert. What do you say?"

The thoughts of singing with the choir actually did sound like fun to her. As he'd said, she didn't have to do it longer than a few weeks, if she decided it wasn't for her. "When are the tryouts?"

He laughed. "Tryouts? Who are we? No tryouts. Show up and sing. 10:30 tomorrow morning. The songs should be ones you're already familiar with. You can grab a choir robe when you get here."

When she took a seat again, she sat next to Perrin.

"So you've been going to church here since you moved to town?" he asked her.

He handed her the community bread loaf and she tore off a piece, thanking him as she nodded. "It's a nice parish. I haven't been here long, but, when life gives me a lot to think about, this is the place I like to be."

He smiled. "Never thought about it that way. But you're right. I feel at peace here. I haven't thought much about how badly I've needed that for the past few years. In California, it's easier to be...alone...even when you're surrounded with people."

CC let out a small gasp, startled by words that fit inside her like a piece she hadn't realized was even missing before. Back in the city, she'd found herself surrounded with people as work yet feeling completely alone. Moving to a small community, she was still alone because it was in her nature to be uncertain how to make friends. Yet she had made a few friends, mainly through the church and the parishioners she'd met. "I know what you mean. That's how I felt in Boston."

Perrin smiled at her again.

Hours later, after she'd helped clean up, she drove into her driveway. Glistening snowflakes fell silently through the evening. *It's too nice to go in,* she thought. Leaving her car, she walked slowly along the peaceful lane from her house to the shores of the lake. Luckily, the ground wasn't slippery. Snow crunched under her boots.

Talking with Perrin all through dinner had made her realize Sterling Lakes was her opportunity to find a community where she could belong. Although she'd forever teased herself about being Miss Independent, moving to a small town had been the action of a woman looking for a place and people to call home. Maybe she'd agreed to sing in the choir because JB had been a step away from getting down on his hands and knees to beg her, but maybe she'd really enjoy it. She needed to get out more anyway.

But she hadn't moved to Sterling Lakes to find friends or even a home. Her reason stung and she'd tried to hide even from herself about what prompted her transfer. When her boyfriend, Bobby, had broken up with her a little more than six months ago, she'd realized just how empty her life was. He said he'd fallen out of love with her...and in love with someone else. She knew exactly who he'd chosen instead of her. A woman who was her exact opposite: Girly, feminine, always looking like she'd stepped right out of the pages of a magazine. He'd flirted with the precinct receptionist every day-- many times right in front of her.

CC had been humiliated because Bobby always made her feel uncomfortable about how little she cared about wearing fashionable clothes, looking picture perfect even when she was at home, relaxing for an evening. Ever since they'd gotten romantically involved in college, he'd ragged on her about her appearance. *I'm a tomboy. I'm me in all my unkempt glory. And apparently that's not what men want, including someone who's been my best friend as long as I can remember and someone I thought accepted me for who I am.*

When it was over and Bobby had finished delivering his cruel, unexpected Dear John letter, she'd felt like she was suffocating. *Maybe because I knew for so long things weren't right between us, that he wasn't happy with me, even though I'd always liked him just the way he was. Only then could I see that he'd spent years trying to change me. He started that right from the beginning of our romance. But I let it slide. You can't teach an old dog new tricks. I thought he was joking, or at least I told myself he was. I was happy with myself.*

She'd fooled herself with her conviction that Bobby was different from other men for far too long. Running away and finding a new beginning had been impossible at work, since she and Bobby and his new girlfriend all worked in the same precinct. She'd requested a transfer to another department. Not seeing each other every day had helped but not enough.

One particular depressing day, she'd gone for a long drive, reevaluating her situation, and passed by the beautiful cottage. For the first time, she could imagine a different life for herself. *One where I don't need a man or love or anything like those things. I don't need someone who can't love me for who I am, who loves me less when I don't look the way he wants me to. I realized I could find a life where I could blame* him *for being so superficial. Our breakup was based on his issue, not mine. Alone, I don't have to wonder constantly what's wrong with me, why I wasn't beautiful enough for him.*

Odd how having one's confidence shattered could throw up every fence. CC had bordered herself in so no one could touch her. She didn't have to invest any part of herself in what could get her hurt. *As for what could make life worth living...* She'd avoiding dating, but in truth she hadn't met a single man since Bobby made her look at herself differently that made her want to do anything but keep a polite distance.

*Until today.* She was bothered by how much she'd enjoyed talking with Perrin tonight. They had far too many things in common for comfort. He was easy on the eyes, and that sure didn't help. But she didn't want to like him the way she already knew she did. Too much. *He's in town to do his part on church renovations. Remember that. He'll be long gone, back to California, in no time. Just passing through.*

She headed back to her house. Everything looked so clean and fresh, brand new. If only life could be like that--a clean slate, a blank page.

Unnerved, she wondered if the fact that Perrin was just passing through made him safe...or even more dangerous.

"Let me see it in the daylight." CC grabbed Patty's hand over the colorful Gerber daisy and fern arrangement on the dining table the next morning.

Sunshine streamed into the cozy chintz room of Patty's B&B, where the aromas of coffee, pancakes, sausage, and bacon wafted through the air. Nearby, a crackling, spirited fire danced in the fireplace. Evergreen boughs graced the mantle.

"Get your sunglasses," Patty said with a girlish giggle, "it's really bright."

"That's quite a rock, Patty." CC looked at her friend thoughtfully. "Congratulations. I'm really happy for you and Elwood."

"Thanks. Would you consider being one of my bridesmaids?"

CC blinked at her. "Seriously?"

"Seriously."

While they'd become friends since she'd moved in, she couldn't have anticipated such an honor. "Thank you. I'd love to, Patty. I've never been a bridesmaid before. What do I do?"

"Stand with me in a beautiful--but not beautiful enough to outshine mine--dress."

CC laughed. "I can do that. Have you set a date yet?"

Patty nodded. "June 21st. Father Greene said there won't be any problem with him performing the ceremony that day, even though he'll be heading to Ireland on vacation soon after."

"Wonderful."

"I better get back."

When Patty disappeared into the kitchen, CC glanced out the window, feeling restless. She couldn't help being envious of Patty. Her future was bright. Decided. *I have no idea where the future will take me...beyond choir practice.*

CC chuckled inside herself, trying to break up the doom and gloom gathering in her chest. Patty had been surprised she was considering joining the choir, commenting on how she was such a private person. When CC protested at the implication that she was anti-social, she'd ultimately admitted she was. And she wanted to change that.

"'Morning."

The voice pulled her attention away from the winter wonderland outside the window of the Victorian B&B. Perrin stood at her table, fresh scrubbed and glowing, ready to face the day. He pulled out the chair next to her and sat down.

"Mhm, something smells good," she commented, breathing in woodsy masculinity.

"Breakfast. Do you usually have breakfast here?"

"Sometimes, like today. But I meant your cologne. It's nice."

He smiled, pleased with the compliment. "Thanks, but nothing competes with the smell of coffee in the morning."

"I can't disagree with you there."

He reached for a cup and offered to refill hers. CC shook her head. "I wish I could stay, but I've already had breakfast. I need to get going."

"Where are you headed so early, if you don't mind telling me?"

"Mass is at 11."

He glanced at his watch. "You'll be way early. Sure you can't have another cup of coffee first?"

"Actually, JB talked me into joining choir--temporarily. I'm not sure if I'll stick with it past the Christmas program. But I have to go early to practice with them."

"Choir is great. St. Augustine said singing is an elevated form of prayer."

CC gasped a laugh. "Well, that feels like a lot of pressure!"

They shared the amusement, and he said, "I visited Italy for a while. After my dad died. He was stationed there for seven months. While I was there, I went to Mass, which was fascinating."

"It sounds like it."

"I don't eat breakfast most days. Want a ride to church? I planned to go to Mass myself." He drank coffee in-between standing and pulling on his coat and scarf.

"It's so early. Are you sure--?"

"I'm sure. And I'm coming back here later, since I'm staying here, so I can get you back to your car."

"Well, okay. That'd be great." Standing, she shrugged on her coat.

Outside, they hopped into his mid-sized rental. Perrin edged the vehicle away from the B&B, down the pine tree-lined lane to the main road.

"It got really cold last night, but it was so beautiful. Have you been over to see Lake Epiphany?" she asked.

He grinned. "I did. One of my favorite parts of Sterling Lakes."

"It's gorgeous at night. I went to the lake near my house last night, after I got home." She studied the lines of his face, his strong jaw and firm profile, all crowned with thick, dark hair. His strong hands, rested on the steering wheel, were powerfully in command even though relaxed. His tapered fingers reminded CC of an artist who had visited her ceramics class in high school. Whatever silly rumors Patty had heard about him, he seemed to have a quiet strength about him CC found irresistible. Even when he wasn't talking, he radiated a warm and inviting presence.

"You went to relax and enjoy the scenery?" he asked.

She shrugged, glancing away. "Actually, I was kind of keyed up."

"Impending holidays can do that to a person."

"They do tend to dredge up a lot of stuff."

"True, and I've found that it doesn't matter if you're far from that 'stuff'. It always finds you anyway."

When he glanced at her, she saw a hint of sadness in his gaze that bothered her more than it should have. *We both have stuff--a past that haunts us, no matter where we go. But he's just passing through.*

"We can always make new memories, can't we?" she asked, quietly reflective.

"Sure. Of course."

Why did she hear the words 'If only that could make the past disappear' behind his almost too bright words?

"Are you making fun of me?" she asked teasingly.

He chuckled so the crinkles around his beautiful eyes made her heart feel squeezed in wondrous agony, as if it was waking up from being numb for longer than she wanted to remember. "Never. Not me. 'least not until I've heard you sing."

CC gasped and burst out laughing almost simultaneously. She couldn't remember the last time she felt so light and happy, and she told herself it was why she was floored when she saw the ghost of tears in his eyes.

But he was turning away, concentrating on pulling into the church parking lot and an open space. "I wanna show you something," he said, belying the emotional overload she'd seen threatening to break out of him a moment earlier. While she knew they didn't know each other well enough for him to confide in her, she wanted to understand what could bring him so close to the edge like that.

Once out of the car, she shivered in the cold and quickly followed him into the church to a prominent area near the front. "This spot is for the baptismal font."

"That's the stand for it?" She pointed to a rectangular block standing up from the floor.

"Um-hmm. The new font is going right on top of that. Initially, I wanted the entire thing to be from one solid piece of granite, but that didn't work."

"Why not? It sounds lovely."

He shrugged. "It's not financially feasible, unfortunately, and considering the time constraints. But I wish it were. To me, one piece symbolizes the unity of the body and the Spirit in baptism."

"I get that. It's a beautiful image...or would be. But I understand why you can't do something you're not going to be paid to do, right? Like you said, it's financially infeasible." Perrin swallowed noticeably, and she instantly worried she'd insulted him. "Honestly, Perrin, I know nothing about any of this. If I offended you, I'm sorry. I didn't intend to. I think, whatever you do, it'll be beautiful. Honestly."

"Thanks. But...it's been bothering me, and I think that's why I wanted to show you this. Because I wanted to say it out loud, where I couldn't hide behind numbers and logic."

He seemed to be thinking deeply, and she didn't dare interrupt him.

"Everything I learned, I learned from my father before he died," he managed. "Masonry is the continuity of life, of generations, and of God's love. All of that could be symbolized in a one-piece font. My name, Perrin, actually means 'stone'. Did you know that?"

"No. Wow."

"Yeah. Well, that's how much a part of me my family, this profession, and our faith is. Everything is of God. I believe that, just like my father did. He'd say time and money aren't why we do this. At the end of the day, it's all about integrity, giving yourself to the Rock of Life. Maybe it sounds strange, but I had a vision of what this baptismal font should be from the start but, when I started crunching the numbers, I couldn't make it work. So I started thinking of alternative methods that could get the job done." He shook his head. "None of the corners I'd need to cut feel right to me. Not for this place. Not for the vision I have in mind. I need to do this. I need to do it *right.*"

*He confided this in* me. *Not Father Greene. Not Cascade or the other crew involved in the renovations. Me. Why me? And he sounds like he's willing to foot the bill all on his own--or do something wildly creative--to see this happen as well as put in whatever time is required to make his vision come to life. Wow. Just wow.*

CC felt warm. Softly with not a small bit of awe, she said, "I can hardly wait to see what you come up with, Perrin."

He grinned, letting out a deep sigh of relief. "Neither can I."

# *Chapter 4*

Rushing into the parish hall, CC followed the sound of music and headed toward the room where choir practice was being held. Hopefully, her cheeks weren't too red from her close encounter with the fabulous kind.

Dead honest, she liked everything about Perrin Stafford. His sense of humor, his talent, his intelligence, his integrity. His smile. Most of all, he'd impressed on her that he was brave on every level.

*What happened to Miss Independent?* CC couldn't fool herself about that part anymore. She'd been reeling from a breakup that came out of nowhere and staying safe had been critical to preventing total disintegration.

*I wanted a clean slate. Moving to Sterling Lakes provided that. I wasn't interested in any of the guys I've met here. Why did I have to meet Perrin? Especially because he's got a job to do in town, and then he's gone.*

While she was the last person to put any stock in rumors, she'd also learned in her profession that where there was smoke, there was usually fire, too. If Perrin Stafford really was a lady's man, he wasn't looking for more than a passing fancy.

Having her boyfriend dump her so unceremoniously had taught her at least one thing: She wasn't interested in being anyone's passing fancy. But there was no point in writing the future so far in advance. The fact was, she didn't really know Perrin well, so making assumptions--certainly taking any real stock in gossip--was premature and foolish. It was a new morning. She was ready to join the world again, venture out, make friends, and take a risk, even with her heart.

She was getting ahead of herself though. He hadn't actually given any definitive signs he was interested in anymore more than friendship. *So...one day--one* step--*at a time.*

She found the room and slipped inside. A seat with a music book and folder on it at the far end of the circle of about thirty singers was set up with a choir robe draped over the back.

No one paused as she slipped into her robe and took her seat. She recognized the song they were rehearsing and joined in with her high, strong soprano. At the front conducting, JB looked her way and gave her a welcoming wink.

She barely used the materials she'd been given during the practice, already knowing all the songs they rehearsed, luckily. She wasn't quite sure what she'd do with all the stuff in the folder, and organization wasn't much of a skill for her.

When practice was over, JB officially welcomed her as a temporary member of the choir. Though she would rehearse with them and join them for Mass this morning to get used to the group, she'd agreed only to stay until after the Christmas program.

CC was mobbed with friendly, smiling faces just before they moved as a group to the church hall, which had been sectioned off where renovations were taking place.

Peering out into the crowd, she spotted Perrin sitting with Patty. She smiled nervously, taking a deep breath, and he grinned, giving her a double thumbs-up for encouragement. For a moment, it felt as if they were the only two in the room. Then Father Greene approached him, whispering something and motioned to the stack of collection baskets.

Laura Matthewson, the town librarian and part-time fashion model, turned toward to her while they were waiting for the parishioners to trickle in before the service started. "Are you nervous?" she asked. Her luxurious, dark, flowing hair contrasted strikingly against the red choir robe.

Though CC hadn't felt full-on nervous before, seeing the elegant woman next to her, she was abruptly aware that her thick, platinum blond curls were probably disheveled and more than a little untidy. *As usual.* She hadn't expected to see Perrin and she had too much to do this morning for more than a touch of eyeliner and a comfortable outfit since she knew she'd be wearing the choir robe over it. She'd also forgotten to put on lipstick. *As Bobby used to remind me constantly. He always said I was a tomboy, that I need to try harder to be attractive and feminine. I know his new girlfriend spends hours every single day on her appearance.*

Uncomfortable in her own skin now, wondering if Perrin had been thinking she looked like a hot mess earlier, CC fumbled to admit to Laura over the loud conversations of newly arriving worshippers, "I don't do too many group activities."

The librarian didn't seem to notice her discomposure. "Me neither. JB cornered me after the crisis about the water last summer and convinced me to join the choir. I admit, he certainly convinced enough of us to actually make a choir again. Apparently, numbers have dwindled so much in the last few years, Father Greene was starting to talk about disbanding."

CC offered a smile of surprise. "I heard about that situation with the lakes last summer. It was right after I moved in. Pro baseball star--"

"Cliff Markham," Laura filled in.

"Yeah. He headed up the fundraiser and that was really successful, wasn't it?" The wheels in CC's head were turning. While she was in awe that Perrin might actually be considering funding the granite needed for the baptismal font out of his own pocket, maybe there was a way to raise the money another way. "Do you know if Cliff will be coming back to Sterling Lakes anytime soon?"

Laura's face turned a lovely shade of pink. "Yes. He's...actually, he's my boyfriend. He's coming back for the holidays. I wish Christmas was tomorrow." She laughed, blushing again.

Clearly the relationship was a long-distance one and Laura missed him horribly, if the heart she was wearing on her sleeve was any indication. "Do you think he'd be interested in doing any other fundraisers for church renovation? I was talking to Perrin Stafford this morning, and he was telling me how expensive it is to get a single block of granite. There must be some way to raise the money he needs for that so he doesn't have to compromise his vision for the baptismal font."

"I'm sure Cliff would be willing. So...is there anything going on between you and Perrin? I'm sorry for putting you on the spot, but I noticed you two sat together at the potluck last night."

"And everyone's been talking about it since?" CC guessed.

Laura grinned, chuckling. "Yeah, something like that. You have to understand, CC, that a lot of us grew up knowing Perrin. Even though we haven't seen him since we were kids, I inadvertently kept up with him by reading newspapers from all over the country at the library. After he returned from Afghanistan, there was a write-up about him. I was so sorry when I saw the obituary for his wife, who lost her battle with cancer two years ago. My friend Cascade Preston also told me some stuff she'd learned because she'd met up with him again at that point in her work--they did some church renovation jobs together. I just can't imagine how hard losing someone like that must be. He was a good guy, such a strong Christian. He came from a family strong in the faith. Anyway, I hope it works out."

The organist was quietly playing a prelude to the opening hymn.

CC's mind was on what she'd heard about Perrin. Patty had said there was gossip about Perrin being a playboy in California, but how did that fit with being a grieving widower, let alone a strong Christian? In this case, maybe gossip really was just blowing smoke because no one had anything better to do.

*We don't know each other well enough for me to ask something like that yet, even though I could easily find out about his wife in the newspapers Laura read--public knowledge. But that feels shady. Maybe if I tell him my idea about fundraising for the granite, we can get to know each other better and he'll tell me on his own.*

As much as CC loved being involved in the singing at Mass, turning occasionally to seek out Perrin, whose eyes were twinkling at her, she wanted to know more about the situation Laura had brought up at the last minute before the service started.

During the Offertory, there was a break before they started another hymn and the parishioners were talking freely amongst themselves. CC leaned close to Laura and said, "Perrin's wife died of cancer two years ago?"

Laura nodded. "They were married for quite a while. He joined the military right after high school, never expecting to be a war, I'm sure. But he met Diane and then he was called to Afghanistan. He was there for most of the early years of their marriage. When he returned to California, where she lived on the military base, he'd been honorably discharged and apparently they were ready to really start their lives together. But she found out she had cancer and it'd already progressed to late-stage. She was gone within months."

CC's heart ached at what that kind of sorrow must have done to him. Being in the military, he'd had to do his duty when he was called upon, but to come back ready to really start his marriage only to lose his wife almost immediately-- "That's just awful."

Laura nodded.

The cantor announced the Offertory hymn, and CC turned to the page in the hymnal, blinking away tears that blurred her vision. Her own silly breakup with Bobby seemed unworthy of the agony she'd been through compared to Perrin's horror. Closing her eyes, she prayed, *Thank You for guiding me here, Lord. Please make me more compassionate, more caring of others. Let Your loving Spirit fill me with hope, not self-pity and small mindedness.*

Looking out to the congregation, she saw Perrin helping with the collection baskets on the aisle nearest her. A strange thought occurred to her. Maybe she hadn't run away from Boston and Bobby's breakup to hide so much as to be here, where maybe God wanted her to be. For Perrin.

The thought was anything but comforting, especially when she saw Perrin moving ever closer--to the collection table at the far end of the sanctuary. But, a moment later, her compassion and respect won out for what he must have endured. Being back in Sterling Lakes would be good for him. Maybe he'd derive comfort from being here, where he'd grown up so happily. She'd gotten that impression talking to him last night. Sterling Lakes felt like home to him, more so than California ever had.

That reminded her of their meeting, how he'd come around wanting to tour the house he'd grown up in. Maybe she could bring that up--if he stuck around, right after Mass.

On their way back to the choir practice room to stash their music and robes, Laura said, "You did fantastic. JB was wise to recruit you. You have a beautiful voice. I hope you'll come back Thursday night at 7 to join us again."

"How late does it usually go?"

"Nine most times."

CC nodded. JB thanked her again as she made her way out to the sanctuary, her heart on wings. She spotted Patty, Elwood, and Perrin and made a beeline for them. They all complimented her singing, claiming they could actually hear her about the others, which she doubted. Perrin said he'd brought earplugs just in case. But he hadn't needed them. She laughed, not minding the teasing because they were genuinely complimenting her for her courage or her voice.

"Are you kids up for going out?" Patty asked. "Elwood's invited me to brunch over at his country club. You missed breakfast, Perrin. You must be starving. CC?"

"Thanks for the offer, but I'll have to pass. I need to get back."

"Unfortunately, I have to as well," Perrin said, and CC's stomach did somersaults at the hope that he'd refused the offer because he wanted time alone with her.

Once the older couple took off, CC slipped into her coat, looping her sparkly scarf around her shoulders as she asked as casually as possible, "Were you serious? Do you have something else to do? Because I was kind of hoping maybe you'd like to come over and get that tour of your old house. We can grab my car on the way and meet at my cottage. I can whip up lunch for us, if you're interested. And I had some ideas about how we can raise money for the granite you need for the font."

"Now that sounds interesting...and too good to pass up. How can I refuse?"

The low sound of his husky voice held warmth that, contradictorily, gave her the shivers. He was looking at her the same way, studying her face and clearly liking what he saw, though she hadn't spent hours (not even ten minutes, in all honesty) trying to beautify herself today.

"Singing obviously agrees with you. Your cheeks are pink, your eyes are bright, and you seem happy," Perrin commented as they made their way outside, arms touching, through the crowds in the parking lot.

*I'm not sure singing gave me all that. But okay.* "I'm sure my old boyfriend would disagree," she said once they were inside his rental again. "I had to get an early start today--earlier than usual--so I didn't spend much time on my appearance. He used to tell me all the time I wasn't doing enough to be attractive for him."

"What a jerk," Perrin grunted without mincing words. "Especially since you're not a woman who needs to do spend laborious hours on making yourself beautiful. You're that naturally."

Her face flamed in pleasure, and she wound a strand of admittedly tangled hair around her finger, trying to calm herself. "My hair's always a mess. And I don't wear makeup, or enough of it."

"Your hair is pleasantly windswept, and you don't need makeup, CC. Honestly, I thought you were gorgeous with powdered sugar all over your face, wearing a stained apron."

She couldn't help laughing in astonishment at his words. "Um...you mean I had powdered sugar on my face when you showed up unannounced on my doorstep last night?"

"Oh, yeah. Whole streaks of it." He gestured wildly with his hands, implying she'd been wearing a face full of the sweet stuff. That he was being dramatic told her she'd had some--and no one else had mentioned it later during the potluck, so it couldn't have been too much.

She moaned but also giggled despite her humiliation, and he laughed heartily. "You were adorable. I wouldn't've changed a thing. Your boyfriend was a creep, and you're better off without someone so superficial...someone who obviously couldn't see the treasure he had while he had it."

CC swallowed, awed because Perrin seemed to like her for how she was--powdered sugar, stained apron, tousled hair, lipstick-less mouth and all. But she found herself agreeing with his assessment, "I'm just beginning to realize how much I'm better off without him."

# *Chapter 5*

Very few things in Perrin's life had prepared him for the emotions that assailed him when he pulled up to the old homestead. He'd dropped CC off to get her car and driven straight here. When he'd been at her cottage yesterday, it'd been dark and he couldn't see things as vividly.

For a long minute, he couldn't escape the feeling that he was twelve again. He could almost see his father out by the oak tree at the far end of the lawn, weeding the flowerbed with all the varieties of annuals and perennials he'd planted to surprise his wife for their anniversary that year. The blooms had been in full, glorious color under the bright sun.

At the other end of the yard, barely visible from the front of the house, his mother stood pulling clothes off the clothesline. Flapping the sheets and pillowcases in the summer breeze, she folded each carefully while the same breeze that'd dried the clothes made the hem of her dress dance.

Scampering across the side yard were the inseparable family dogs, one Golden and one Irish Setter. They'd been found by his dad at a job site when they were just pups. Perrin's brother Tim tossed sticks their way while their little sister Annie played in the grass with a small, pink bucket. Her cat dozed by her side.

Perrin got out of his car, moving toward the front porch. The number of times he and his dates had sat on the porch swing and talked...and kissed after they'd spent time with his family were happy memories. He'd had a few girlfriends and all had been serious enough to meet his parents. Still, none like Diane. His whole family had fallen in love with her, and he'd always been grateful for that, considering how quickly he'd been called to duty in Afghanistan after their wedding. Diane hadn't been completely alone those long years of separation because she'd had his family to remind her of their love.

Hearing a car pull into the driveway and park, he turned to watch CC get out and walk toward him. He wondered if she'd ever known tragedy. He hoped not. But life had a way of changing on a dime. Happy times could be gone in an instant. Death and tragedy, hardship and loss were a part of life, and Perrin had tried his hardest not to allow that to taint his faith, but he hadn't been entirely successful.

The mashing of a Bible version came back to him: *God never gives us a burden that's heavier than what we're able to carry.* How often had Diane said that near the end? She'd always assured him the fact that they got up every morning was a win, and he'd believed it until that first morning when he'd woken up alone. All he'd wanted to do was give up. What was the point of going on? His absence in her life for so long while he was a soldier had felt like a punishment to him instead of a respected obligation.

*Just when she needed me most. My punishment for abandoning her after we got married was her permanent absence from my life. Just when I needed her most.*

"Do you want to walk around the grounds or go in and have lunch first?" CC asked, and he mentally shook himself out of his dark thoughts. Fortunately, it wasn't hard to come into the light when CC looked so happy and irresistible. He joined her in an easy smile while looking around nostalgically.

"I lost track of the number of times me and my brother shoveled the driveway over the years. Dad wasn't one for investing in time-saving, expensive equipment. We had trusty shovels and...we learned to appreciate the hard work later. Much, much later."

CC giggled at his reminiscing. He pointed to the small garden near the front of the house. "That's the rose bush my dad planted for my mom on their 10th anniversary."

"The blooms were gorgeous when they bloomed. Such a pretty coral color."

"What's your favorite part of the cottage so far?" he asked.

"Too many things. I fell in love with it as soon as I saw it. I had to buy it. When I first moved here last summer, I came outside every evening, even when it rained, and sat on the porch swing. I loved that. So peaceful. It was hard to stop doing it, but it's been too cold. I can't wait for the weather to turn nice so I can do that again."

"The swing was one of my favorite parts of the house, too."

In his mind's eye, Perrin saw his mom in a white apron and yellow shirt dress, a tall glass of lemonade in one hand, sitting in her rocker on one side of the porch, cooling down in the evening after the mid-afternoon heat. His dad would be stretched out on the hammock nearby, reading the newspaper. When the rest of the family joined them just beyond the porch so they could look up at the stars, his father would point out the positions of the constellations, asking if anyone could name them.

"Maybe you'll come over when the weather is nice again. If you're around." CC's breath was white from the cold.

"I'd love that. Let's go in now. It's too cold to be dawdling."

"I'm fine. I don't mind. I don't have blue lips yet."

"That you know of?"

She gave him a scolding grimace that ended on a smile, then unlocked the front door. "Whenever you're ready," she invited.

*She's giving me time and space to see the past, unobstructed,* he realized.

He stepped into the cozy vestibule. "Do you mind if I take a look in the closet?" he said, pointing to the faceted glass doorknob on the coat closet.

"Sure. What's in there? Other than the few unremarkable and unfashionable coats and shoes I own?"

He opened the door, peering inside along the right side of the doorframe. When she joined him, she also saw the height markings and dates for all of them in his mother's neat printing. CC glanced at him, her bright blue eyes warm. "I never noticed that before."

"My mom even measured when we could first sit up."

Her gaze moved from the lowest marking to the tallest--which mean she had to crane her neck a little both ways. Both Perrin and his brother ended up as tall as their dad.

"I'm glad it didn't get painted over," she said with genuine happiness.

"So am I."

Aware that he was breathing in the clean scent of soap at her nearness a little too deeply and noticing how nice her mouth was even without the lipstick her stupid old boyfriend had claimed was missing, he had no wish to move. Ever again. She was a few feet shorter than him, not slight and not in any way bulky. *Perfect. And she would feel about perfect in my arms, too...*

"How about that lunch? And hot chocolate? I'm having a craving. Are you in?" she asked, maybe to cover the pause that had gone on too long while he thought about things that made him marvel.

"Oh, yeah." *All in.* The impulsive thought both surprised and pleased him as much the desire to hold her had.

"Good. Join me whenever you're ready." She ducked out of the closet and disappeared from his sight.

*Diane would like her.*

The thought should have been anything but comforting, yet something about it *was*. Impossibly was. Diane had lived on the base where he'd been stationed in California while he was in Afghanistan. Although she'd liked the people on the base and his family off it, she'd often said the other people they'd known in California didn't seem quite authentic. Everyone seemed to have a façade in place, one that became "who they were". A time or two, she'd wondered if they even knew themselves who they were deep down. Being herself was what Diane as all about, just like CC obviously was.

Left to his own devices, Perrin viewed the living room with its crank-out windows still in place, giving the room a Gothic feel. From his memories, he could clearly see the holiday tree decorated exuberantly on the hearth in front of the fireplace, and all the wrapping paper littering the carpet willy-nilly Christmas morning during gift-opening. He saw Tim in his pajamas with a new cowboy hat and holster. Annie squealing with delight over the new pink tricycle she rode around the empty garage during the day while their dad was at work with the car, since the driveway had always had too much snow and ice on it in the winter.

In place of the corner table where their Nativity scene had lovingly been placed every Christmas was a different table with a yellow lamp and a magazine. The room itself was also sparse now without photographs, plants, toys or discarded shoes his parents were always tripping over.

"Lunch is ready," CC called from the kitchen. He turned and went immediately, just like he had when his mom had done the same long ago.

CC had made a plate of sandwiches, put out a bowl of chips with a jar of pickles, and steaming mugs of cocoa sat in front of plates waiting to be filled. "Hope you don't mind simple. I really need to get groceries. Terrible time to realize that, but I hope you like turkey and Swiss."

"Love both. Simple is the mainstay of my life," he assured her, giving Bella a stroke on her barstool. She purred at him lovingly. "Thanks for doing this. The really nice thing about coming here for this job is that I haven't had to eat alone even once. And being *here*--this house--for a meal again... Anyway, thanks. Many a lunch, we had something just like this growing up."

They sat, filled their plates, and ate companionably for a few minutes before he asked, "Where's your Christmas tree going?"

She shrugged. "I'm not sure I'm getting one."

Perrin gaped. "What? Why not?"

She chuckled. "Is having one like written in stone with you?"

"Yes!"

She laughed again. "Well, with work and not being home most of the day...it's just for me and Bella..."

"Excuses."

"Valid ones," she defending, and they shared the easygoing rapport with mirth. "Honestly, I don't know if it's worth it. I might just keep things simple."

*Translation: A Christmas tree would make me feel even lonelier?*

Frowning, he wondered what the story was with her idiot boyfriend that she was so much better without. Perrin didn't really know anything about the relationship, so maybe it wasn't as cut and dried as he could dub it without any connection or knowledge. "I really can't imagine not having a Christmas tree at Christmas."

"You do every year, even now as an adult?" she asked.

He paused because he'd been deep in nostalgia when he'd spoken about needing the tree, and now he had to admit, "No, you're right. I guess I haven't had one for at least two years." Swallowing, he took a sip of hot chocolate, realizing he felt like he could and should admit this to her. "Not since my wife died."

"I heard about that," CC said gently.

"Did you?" he asked, astonished. He hadn't talked about it... But it was a small town, and it wasn't as if it was a secret.

"Yeah," she said, cringing a little about the gossip. "I'm so sorry, Perrin. That couldn't have been easy. I can't imagine how anyone gets through something that tough."

"It's been the hardest two years of my life, and I was in a war before that."

"Wow," she said simply.

"Yeah. It's weird, but I haven't really wanted to get over Diane and how devastated I was when cancer took her. I came back here, and... I don't know, but I can't stop thinking that maybe I do need to get on with my life."

"Being here in your old house?" she clarified, "that's what's telling you you're missing life?"

"Yeah. Definitely that. But...it's not the only thing."

It'd been so long since he'd liked a woman as much as he did CC. He hadn't thought about a relationship and romance once since Diane passed, though he'd had plenty of people in California reminding him constantly that he should be thinking about it, that two years was long enough to grieve.

The fact that he was only in Sterling Lakes as long as it took to complete the contract didn't bother him too much. There was no rush--for anything in his life. And that included speaking out loud his hope to get to know CC Cogshell better. He wasn't sure whether or not that would scare her off at this point.

"So where do you want to poke around next?" she asked him casually, but he saw the pretty pink color in her cheeks.

*Does she like me, too? But she's not ready to do anything to jinx it? Better to let nature take its course, slow and easy.*

"I'd love to see the attic again."

"Sounds like a plan. Honestly, I've barely been up there since I toured the house, thinking about buying it. The second floor had all the storage I needed when I got here, but I admit I loved the gorgeous view from up there that first time. I've thought about doing something with it--later, when I have more time and money."

"My parents thought about making it a master suite before we moved out."

"The people I bought the house from said the same thing. I guess that might end up a tradition of the house at this point. So why did your parents move?"

He shrugged. "The economy went downhill here in Sterling Lakes. Clarke's Falls deliberately blocked the water coming into town and the whole place nearly folded with that feud erupted. My dad lost his job. We ended up in California, where Dad got a new job."

"Do you like California?"

"Honestly, no. But it's where I met Diane--my wife. And I just stayed there after I was discharged from the military. Most of my family's still there. Dad died about five years ago, and Mom stayed in California to be near the grandkids."

They'd finished eating. Together, they cleaned up their simple meal, then headed to the second floor.

"Do you know why this town is called 'Sterling Lakes'?" CC asked. "I've wondered since I moved here."

"I did a report on it in the third grade. Legend has it that some of the earliest explorers from the colonial times climbed to the treetops and saw the view of the lakes all strung together, like sterling links on a chain."

"Bet you got an A+ on that report."

"One of my few," he managed with a grin.

On the second level, he ducked into his old bedroom to see it being used as little more than a storage room. Memories assailed him despite the vast differences. He pointed out which of his family inhabited the other rooms, mentioning a few highlights before they reached the door at the end of the hallway.

The steep, narrow staircase up to the attic was lit only by the bare light bulb at the bottom. CC let him pull the string to turn it on. At the top of the stairs, they stood together in the dim, wide, dusty space. The ceiling sloped on both sides, cramping the space a bit. His dad always said that was the reason they didn't make it a master bedroom suite. The ceiling was a problem.

Perrin felt more than a little uncomfortable, not sure how to say what he'd actually come here with the intention of asking. Starting awkwardly, he managed, "CC, I want to ask you something. Before he died, my father told me he left a diary chronicling his army stay in Italy in the 70s along with some love letters to my mom. He was there for four years and had no other contact with my mother except their letters. They got married shortly after he got home with an honorable discharge."

She was still listening, not looking suspicious.

"I know this is a very strange thing to ask for, but would you mind if we rooted around under the floorboards to see if I can find them? He said they were under here somewhere, that he forgot about them during the move, and when he remembered it was too late to go back and try to get them. He said I could read them and decide whether I wanted to give them to Mom. I know she would love to have those letters. I promise, if you find a cash windfall under the boards, it's all yours."

Dawning entered CC's expressed as she seemed to realize now why he'd been so uncomfortable when he showed up on her doorstep last night. Since it sounded a little strange, maybe even creepy, to lead off with a request like that, he hadn't had the guts to go through with it then. But she smiled now, endearing him with her enthusiasm when she said, "Let the treasure hunt begin!"

Perrin wasn't sure if it meant she didn't trust him, but they worked together, moving around the attic, looking for loose floorboards. Finally, they found one, and it took some doing to pry it up. They looked down the black hole together, and CC said, "I'm not putting my hand into that potential spider-infested space."

Perrin guffawed. "Guess it's up to me."

Taking a deep breath, he reached into the dark space below and rooted around gingerly until his hand came in contact with a small stack of papers. He pulled it up, bringing up a plume of dust with them. The fragile-looking, loose pages were bound together with only a rubber band. The writing on them was small and sloping, and Perrin couldn't read a word.

He looked up, and CC leaned forward to flip through them. After a moment, she said, "They're all written in Italian."

He was struck with a thought. "You speak Italian, don't you?"

*Abruzzi, Italy*
*June 2, 1978*

*I'm learning to speak and write Italian and I thought starting a journal of my time stationed in Italy might be a good way to really get to know the language. If I ever get fluent, I might look back at this and wonder if it makes any sense, but here goes:*

Sunshine sparkles on the dancing waves of the Adriatic Sea. The beauty is breathtaking, but I always have to wear my sunglasses whenever I'm crossing the bridge in the military Jeep otherwise I wouldn't be able to navigate the narrow roads that line the cliffs of the Almafi coastline. I love climbing them at the army Jeep's maximum speed.

Only two weeks into my four-year tour here and already I feel like I'm home. Quite a change for a guy who never left my home in Sterling Lakes before and never really wanted to. My signature was all it took to enlist in the army and, with that, a world of possibilities opened up before me. Here, they've placed me on the beautification and reconstruction project of the barracks, where I can put my experience as a stone mason to work.

One regret keeps stabbing at my insides. Leaving Helene and putting our wedding plans on hold. What kind of sacrifice was that to ask her to make? I know it's too much, yet she believes in me, and we believe in our future together.

I still can't believe she agreed to marry me--and after I slipped that puny popcorn ring on her finger. She didn't balk. Instead, she gave me her most joyous smile and hugged me tightly. She acted like it was worth a fortune instead of all I could afford without putting myself in debt before we're actually husband and wife. How did I get so lucky to find a woman so wonderful?

I can't wait to start our future together. Once my tour is done, I can afford to live a good, honest, normal life. That wasn't possible before. The economic outlook was just too bleak. I wanted more for her, for us. My military service will give us what we can't have otherwise. But being apart...I'm not sure how either of us will deal with that. I miss her all the time.

When I come into Abruzzi, bouncing across the ancient cobblestone plaza and to a parking spot in the town square, I'm always drawn to the beauty of the elaborately carved fountain spraying water high in the air. Children and parents stroll and frolic in the June sunshine, and countless birds splash ecstatically there, chirping and singing a joyous welcome. At the far end is the large cathedral with a high staircase leading up to massive doors. That church is so beautiful, it could be a postcard--and probably is. I wish Helena could be here to see it with me. There's so much charm and natural beauty in this place. She would love it here.

But I have to get to work. The masonry studio can't be too far. The sheet my commanding officer gave me has the address. As I look around to orient myself, I'm also thinking about a nice spot to have my lunches. The plaza is lined with bright awnings delineating shops, boutiques, cafes, and souvenir stands.

Suddenly all around me, the deafening chimes of church bells clang. I look over my shoulder to see the cathedral. Most of the folks in the town square are frozen in place, just like I am. The spire of the bell tower rises far up into the sky. I can feel the vibrations of the bells all through my body, and I get chills at the unforgettable experience.

I have to see the church up close. I walk across the plaza and find myself a few minutes later at the foot of a massive staircase. I'm not the only one there. Others have also gathered in this spot to admire the cathedral.

The stonework on the staircase is surely centuries old, and I note the words 'San Marco' etched in the stone repeatedly. That's when I realize I'm standing in front of the Cathedral of San Marco, looking at stonework masons and artisans like me crafted generations earlier.

Awe overwhelms me, and I say a silent prayer: *Guide me, Lord, to where I can serve best.*

"Hello, sir. Excuse me."

I hear the soft, melodic Italian voice behind me.

"Please, sir."

Turning, I find a young woman, her dark hair dancing and her skirt fluttering in the breeze. Her pale skin seems to glow in the brightness of the day, lending her a fragility that reminds me of a butterfly.

"Please," she says again, and I'm aware then that she's actually yelling over the sound of the bells. At last the final chime of the "Ave Maria" sounds, resonating in the air. Only then do I speak. "Good day, miss. I am American." My Italian is rough, but she seems to understand me. It's a language I understand when written better than I can speak it...but that's not saying much.

"Yes, yes, friend, soldier." Her bright eyes sparkle.

"Friend. Ted." I shake her hand then point to the name emblazoned on my uniform. "Ted Stafford."

"Ted, Ted Stafford," she repeats, the points to herself. "Maria Bianco. Italian. Good. Thank you, Ted Stafford."

I admit it, I can't take my eyes off her. The sound of her voice is like the bells that continue to chime in the background. There's something otherworldly about her with her shiny, beige shoes and bright red purse. "Maria."

"Friend."

Suddenly, a matronly woman in a buttoned-up blue trench coat rushes up to us and grips Maria by the elbow. "Excuse me, my dear!"

"Mamma?"

"Maria, stay with the group!" the woman scolds.

Looking confused, Maria's gaze holds mine. "Tomorrow, Ted. Goodbye," she says before allowing the woman to hustle her off into the crowd.

I consider following them, but they disappear into the noontime throng crowding the plaza and then I wonder why I would even think to follow. But I can't lie to myself. Maria appeared like a vision before me, and I can't get her out of my head, even when I know I have to.

But the walk back down to the plaza has my mind throwing questions out like confetti. Who is she? Where did she come from? Why did that woman hustle her off with such urgency, as if Maria is an escaped convict she has keep in check?

An odd thought strikes me then. Does Maria need help? Is she in trouble? Should I have followed her after all?

The image of Maria's lovely cameo-like profile comes into his mind's eye over and over. No, there hadn't seemed to be anything in her demeanor or expression to indicate she was in danger or needed help.

She called that woman "mamma", I recall. Maybe the older woman is an overprotective parent?

Whatever. It isn't my problem. At the newspaper stand, I show the clerk the address for the masonry studio. Lots of arm waving follows with the friendly clerk communicating in very broken English.

The studio is apparently around the plaza in the opposite direction from where I came, on the side of the street with 'le mare'--the sea.

Back in my Jeep, I have to stop to let some pedestrians pass, noticing a woman with a baby stroller. She looks like a painting of the Madonna, just the way I imagine Helene will look when she's out for a walk with our first baby.

I can't help missing my Helena again, wishing I could tell her everything that's happened to me on my Italian odyssey.

The first turn I take leads me down a winding dirt path lined with scrubby fir trees. No way can this be right, I think. These stone workers have to get their materials to the studio. The road is barely passable.

Shifting into reverse, I emerge from the woods and get back on to the main route I was on before, only to find what I'm looking for twenty minutes later. 'Stuioia Pierreino' is written on a small sign on the roadside that I might have missed if I was going any faster.

I pull off the road and follow the wide drive down a steep hill to a sprawling complex that looks utterly deserted. Striding to the front of the building, I find a paper sign fluttering on the door: "Closed due to illness. Thank you. Come back tomorrow," it says.

I rip the sign down, muttering, "You've gotta be kidding me."

*Abruzzi, Italy*
*June 3, 1978*

The next morning, my commanding officer, Captain Greyson, gives me a stony look. "Welcome to Italy, Stafford. What happened to you yesterday happens all the time here. It's a miracle they ever get anything done in this country...this impossibly beautiful country."

"It is magnificent," I concede.

"But we need the expertise of these locals. They've been here for centuries. They know this stone and granite like they know their kid's names. So just go back today and hope for the best."

"Understood. And if they're not there today, sir?"

"We'll cross that bridge when we come to it, Stafford. Remember, we're U.S. Army soldiers."

"Yes, sir." I salute and leave the office.

Stopping at the base post office, I mail the letter to Helene I wrote the night before, explaining everything to her about Abruzzi, the bells, St. Marco Cathedral, and the mason studio being closed.

*Be well, my love.* I toss the letter in the canvas satchel marked 'U.S. ARMY POST.' Hopping into a Jeep, I travel the route I took yesterday, appreciating the beauty of the scenery around me anew.

On the passenger seat is the leather case holding the camera I've been requisitioned to take photos of the stone workings the locals will be showing me. Helena would love to see the Cathedral of San Marco. I figure the detour will only take a moment, and, while I'm there, I can take a few shots of the lettering in the stairs.

Once I park, I glance at my watch. The bells will start chiming in a few moments. I climb the stairs in front of the cathedral then turn to view the vista before me. Stretching as far as the eye can see, the hills of the Abruzzi region roll into the distance until they kiss the blue horizon. I gasp at the grandeur of it all. God designed this. The evidence of His handiwork is irrefutable.

After snapping a few shots of the landscape, I shift my attention to the plaza in front of the cathedral, viewing the crowd beneath me. Milling about or bustling past, each individual has a unique purpose, a special story, and a life path all their own. I consider myself lucky to be part of it.

Then I see her, almost like I've been searching for her. Poised at the edge of the plaza, in almost exactly the same spot as the previous day, stands the beautiful Maria. She has an air of waiting for someone.

*"Tomorrow," she said.*

Is she actually waiting for me? I wonder.

No longer thinking, I hustle down the stairs, knowing how quickly individuals can be swallowed by the crowd. Nearing her, I see that today she wears a lilac cardigan sweater and a billowy, butter cream skirt. With her dark, sleek bob, she resembles a gorgeous, exotic flower.

"Maria," I call.

She turns in my direction, sunlight glinting off the strand of pearls around her snowy neck. Her pallor strikes me once more, lending an unearthly air to her appearance. When she sees me, a broad smile transforms her face from somber sadness to a beacon of joy and hope.

"Ted Stafford," she pronounces in her heavily accented tones, holding her hands out to me.

I can't believe how beautiful she looks. It nearly takes my breath away. "Hello, Maria."

Appreciating her twinkling eyes and lovely appearance, I bring up the camera, asking if she minds if I take a photo of her. She tilts her head to one side and laughingly replies, "Yes, yes."

I snap two shots before the woman I assume to be her mother appears again, takes Maria by the arm, and throws a glare at me. Yet she gestures for me to come closer to them. "Mr. Stafford, my name is Sister Lorenzo. A letter for you from Maria. Maria is very sick." She lowers her voice, tapping her head at the temple area with her index finger.

Not sure what's going on, if I'm misunderstanding the words she said, I reluctantly take the letter she offers me. The breeze picks up then, and I notice she's wearing a nurses' uniform underneath her coat that flaps in the momentarily gusting wind.

She said Maria was sick. I look from one to the other, but my gaze rests on Maria. Resembling a saint from another era, she smiles at me. It's clear to me then: Beautiful Maria is sick in some way, maybe in the head, and Sister Lorenzo is her nurse.

I pat the letter, saying, "Thank you." Lifting the camera again, I ask, "A picture?"

This time, both of them smile, standing arm-in-arm. Once I take a few shots, I say, "Thank you. Goodbye." The world doesn't seem quite real to me, something I can't explain at that moment.

"Goodbye, Ted Stafford," they call.

With a crisp salute, I move through the crowd and back to my Jeep. As I drive from the plaza, I see them both waving goodbye to me. A lump fills my throat so I can barely swallow. What in the world can be wrong with Maria? Was she injured in an accident? Perhaps she'll tell me in her letter.

The real question is, how can I possibly get involved in their lives? I'm a very busy serviceman with a schedule that leaves little or no time for outside activities. Besides, there's another angle I've been warned about by my instructor at basic training. He said all American soldiers in uniform have to be careful about being targeted for schemes by the locals.

I have no way of knowing if Maria is really ill or if Sister Lorenzo is really a nurse. The whole thing might be a set-up. Stranger things happen in life. At least I have a photo of them on the army camera to prove who they are and possibly track them down, if anything shifty comes of this.

But, if they are scamming me, would they have stood there posing for pictures? That would be pretty stupid.

I sigh, unsure what's right. The letter from Maria might answer my questions. I'll have to get someone back at the base to help me translate it, if I can't do it myself, to see if it holds any sort of a clue. I'm still just learning this language so I expect I will need help. The urgency inside me insists I find someone to translate it ASAP. Chaplain Dennis will help me get to the bottom of this. I decide to go to him right after I get back from the masonry studio.

# Chapter 6

CC looked up from silently reading the first two journal entries on the loose pages. While she could read them, they required a lot of guesswork along with translation--both because of his dad's hard-to-read handwriting and what was clearly Italian written by a man who was just first learning how to speak and write in the language. She'd read a few lines to Perrin when they'd first found the loose journal, but--finding out how much work would be involved--he'd asked her to read ahead and sum up instead.

Now that she'd read a little, she said vaguely, "This is very personal, Perrin. I'm not sure I'm comfortable continuing. Did your dad tell you why he wanted you to get the journal and letters?"

"Just before he died, he asked, if I ever came over to Sterling Lakes for any reason, if I'd try to get them from the attic of this house."

CC sighed. She didn't want to be the one to keep the truth from Perrin, let alone to tell him what she was reading and what it implied.

His dad had clearly met another woman, an Italian woman named Maria, while stationed in Italy. The letters hinted at an attraction. Beyond that, she couldn't speculate, not without reading more, and that would take some time. Until she knew more, she didn't want to tell Perrin anything that could make him wonder if his father had been unfaithful to the woman who would become his wife after he was discharged.

Besides... "Does your mom read or speak Italian?"

"No."

"So she'll never know what this diary says unless it's translated?"

"I was hoping I could tell her. You know, after you tell me."

He was smiling, but she felt so awkward, she insisted, "Maybe you should just take the journal and letters--if we find them--back to your mom and not read them." That was what she preferred, for sure.

"He said I could read them, and I'd really like to get an up-close-and-personal view of his time in Italy while he was in the service. Mom would want to know what the journal says."

To say anything would lead to an implication that she wasn't sure was correct. Better to say nothing until she'd read them all and had a better idea of the whole picture. She wished there was a polite way to say she didn't want to read these, end of story. But she understood how important having them translated would be to Perrin and his mom. *Unless this situation ends up not good. Then they won't thank me then. Maybe it would be better that way.*

She forced a bright smile. "Well, why don't we take a break anyway? I can't read all these right now. I'm exhausted, and I've only gotten through two days of the journal. Your dad's new Italian is more than a little rough."

They both stood up, and she felt like her bones creaked on the way up. They both laughed, and it felt good to let go and get away from the stifling journal entries. Although they were written beautifully, so she felt like she was right there with his dad, there was a premonition of sadness she couldn't explain until she knew more.

"I made enough hot chocolate earlier for seconds. Should I heat that up?" she asked as they carefully made their way back down the stairs.

"I love chocolate. Sure."

"Okay." While she went to the stove on the lower floor, he went to the kitchen table to get their mugs from where they'd left them earlier. She noticed how well his dark hair contrasted with the off-white fisherman's sweater. Fighting an urge to hug him, she busied herself at the stove.

"I know this all sounds weird--for me to come back here for the journal and letters--but after I met you, it wasn't just about that. I'd genuinely like to get to know you better, CC."

She swallowed the lump already in her throat. "I'm not really used to that. I didn't grow up with a lot of friends."

"How did you grow up?" he asked, leaning against the counter while she carefully stirred the hot chocolate to remove the skin and bring it slowly back up to a warm temperature.

"My mom died when I was a teenager. After that, my dad was either drunk or gone, working. I had a lot of lonely weekends, holidays. Christmas always seemed like the worst because the rest of the world seemed so happy when I couldn't even imagine."

"That's why you don't have your own Christmas tree," he guessed.

"We never did. I don't remember ever having one, though I suppose we must have when Mom was alive. I found the decorations when Dad and I were moving."

"Sad story," he said genuinely. "I'm sorry, CC."

She nodded, glancing again at the hot chocolate before continuing, "So when I was 17--a senior in high school--Dad remarried a woman with kids younger than me. We moved into her house. That's actually a good thing because he stopped drinking and seemed happier. But...I just never really fit in. There's nothing more to say about that. They never tried, I never tried. When they did notice me, it was to point out what I was doing wrong, not doing what I should be doing, according to them. And to remind me how unfeminine I was. I was always a tomboy. The only friend I ever had was Bobby. We went off to college together. I loved his family. They were military, and...I just was really impressed with their traditions. That was what a family should be like, in my mind. I wanted to belong with them instead of where I was."

She pulled the pan off the heat, then carefully filled the mugs over the sink. A moment later, they were sitting together in the living room, sipping, and she surprised herself when she admitted, "It got romantic between me and Bobby after we both got jobs at the Boston police department as detectives. I admit, I had a crush on him for years and I wanted things to go that way, but I didn't have any confidence in myself. I thought he accepted me the way I was. He didn't comment on my lack of femininity while we were growing up...not until we got involved romantically. Then he was just like everyone else. I was never feminine enough for him. Never good enough. I was blindsided when he told me he fell in love with someone else--the receptionist at the precinct he was always flirting with and she was making eyes at him. I just couldn't believe he would do that to me. I couldn't cope. So I just took off one day and ended up here. This house seemed like the answer to all my prayers. I bought the house, transferred to the Intelligence and International Translation Department, and being away from him every day helped a lot. But being in Sterling Lakes...well, I feel like I'm home for the first time in my life. I don't know if I ever felt like I had a real home before this one."

His gaze on her was kind, sympathetic, and when she finished, he said, "I'm sorry you went through all that. It wasn't fair to you. I'm sure you have enough experience to doubt me when I say this, but I love how refreshingly *you* you are. You *are* the person I met last night. There's no subterfuge. But your boyfriend was wrong-- they were all wrong about how you look. You're beautiful. Whether you're a tomboy or not, you're beautiful just the way you are, as natural as you are. You don't need all that feminine stuff. The fact that you don't care about any of that is so unlike what I'm used to in California, and I suppose that's why I appreciate it so much."

CC saw an opening into asking about those silly rumors going around concerning him. "You have a lot of girlfriends in California?"

He barked a laugh of surprise. "None. There's been no other woman for me since Diane, though it's nice to be hit on as often as I am, I suppose. But my wife was like you--what you see is what you get. And I loved her. Loved everything about her. She was beautiful, too. Even when she was so sick, she hated how she looked, she was lovely to me."

Her heart aching, CC asked softly, "Do you think you'll...? I mean, I understand now how much you loved her and the thought of going on without her couldn't have been easy all this time. But...do you think you'll ever get over her?"

"Before I came here, I wasn't sure. Actually, I was sure. The answer was no. I wasn't getting over her. End of story. Now--"

He looked at her steadily, making her wonder if she had something to do with the change, but her heart warned her not to assume anything. *Don't read into it. Even if you want to.*

"A part of me didn't want to get on with my life," he added, his voice pained. "I didn't want the closure, the healing. Anything that could make me start all over again."

"Because you could lose," she said, not a guess. She understood that. Her situation was nowhere near as drastic as his, but she'd gone through something similar when Bobby betrayed her, proving that he didn't love her for the person she was. He'd loved her for the ideal he wanted her to be and could never live up to. And when he finally admitted to himself she wasn't and never could be his ideal, he'd dumped her.

"Yes," Perrin confirmed. "I don't ever want to go through anything like that again. But...death is a part of life. I've always known that. Accepting it has been the hard part."

For a long moment, they sat in silence, sipping. When he finished, he set his mug on the coffee table before saying, "We haven't found the letters yet--the ones Dad said he and Mom wrote back and forth to each other while he was stationed in Italy. I wonder if they're in the same place as the loose journal was. And I wonder if they're written in Italian."

CC laughed, but her chest felt tight at the thought. "Perrin, why don't you let me read the journal and then I can tell you the gist of it? Or I could actually translate them into English on paper for you."

*What are you doing? Why are you offering this, you soft-hearted fool?*

"That's a lot of work."

"I don't mind."

"I could pay you," he offered eagerly.

She shook her head. "I don't want you to pay me. We're friends, Perrin. I want to help you."

Whether they were good enough friends that he wouldn't be upset if she found out his dad wasn't the man he believed him to be remained to be seen.

CC had breakfast with Patty the next morning at the B&B. While they were drinking a second cup of coffee, Cascade Preston came in. Patty introduced CC before they all sat down.

"Will you be staying long?" Patty asked while pouring her friend coffee.

"Through the weekend. Any room for me here?"

"Always."

"Thanks," Cascade answered. Then her eyes widened when Patty handed her the cup. "What is *that*?"

Patty gave a broad smile. "Elwood popped the question at the potluck supper last night."

"Oh, congratulations, Patty! Let me see that rock up close!"

CC watched the homey scene as Patty and Cascade caught up, but she was tired because she'd been up half the night. After she'd made her stupid offer to translate the loose journal into English, she and Perrin had gone up to the attic and searched for the letters his parents had exchanged, but they hadn't been able to find them under any loose floorboards.

He'd left after that, and she'd been drawn to the diary filled with the intimate, captivating details of Perrin's father's time in Italy. A part of her had hoped she'd gotten the wrong idea before, when she'd read them with Perrin sitting there, watching her too closely. Unfortunately, that would have been too easy. Maria and Ted had fallen in love despite that she had a mental illness and that he already had a fiancée he loved deeply and felt constant guilt for betraying. During the seven months he and Maria had of his four year tour, she started calling him her husband, and his tender, compassionate feelings that were otherwise wholly platonic for the delicate beauty prevented him from forbidding it. Time and time again, he'd told he was already engaged to a woman he cared for and couldn't jilt.

Maria had died suddenly and tragically in a drowning accident. The journal had ended with Ted wondering if Maria had realized and accepted they could never be together--because of the very things that should have prevented them from falling in love in the first place--and she'd committed suicide because she couldn't cope. There was no way he could ever know.

But he'd loved his fiancée, despite the grief for Maria he would silently carry for the rest of his life. He'd intended to go through with the marriage with Helena as soon as he was discharged. Perhaps the most tragic part was that he'd talked to Helena about Maria Bianco, a resident at the San Giovanni Hospital, telling her that he was doing volunteer work there. Helene knew Maria by name, that she'd drowned...but he'd never told her about their feelings for each other before her tragic death.

*Why didn't I just tell Perrin I don't have time to translate the letters? With my job, choir practice, being a bridesmaid for the first time, fixing up my house...*

CC sighed as she considered what had bothered her most of the night after Perrin left. *The journal will hurt him. And I don't want him to be hurt anymore, after what he went through, losing his wife. I don't want him to lose anything good. So I have to find those love letters his parents wrote to each other. If nothing else, maybe they'll soften the blow given when he reads about his dad's tender, chaste love for another woman while he was engaged to Perrin's mom.*

CC had already decided she was going to have some professional work done on the attic, and, if the letters were found in the process, all the better. She and Perrin had had no luck, together, or when she went back up later for a second fruitless search to locate those love letters.

When Patty and Cascade looked at her again to include her in the conversation, CC asked if either of them had any recommendations for a contractor. "I'm thinking of renovating the attic into...well, something. There's such a great view up there. It's a shame no one ever goes up there."

Cascade dug around in her purse. A moment later, she produced a business card. "That attic is fantastic. Here. Russel Vigliani. He specializes in older homes."

"Thanks. How did you know about the view from the attic?"

"Perrin and I were friends when we were little. He's a great guy. I know there are stupid rumors about him, mainly because he lives in California, where apparently all the beautiful women of the world abide, according to the gossip. But he's not like that. I never met his wife, but I know he must have loved her and he's having a hard time getting over her. But I don't know what I'd do without my husband. I don't want to imagine what Perrin must have been through. He's worth whatever effort a woman goes through to help him heal though."

Patty suddenly signaled them, making weird, choking noises that CC finally understood meant Perrin had entered the room and was making his way to their table.

# *Chapter 7*

After initial greetings, Cascade and Perrin hugged and were just starting to get caught up when Cascade received a call and had to run.

"How do you feel about a walk around town, CC? I thought I might walk down to the nearby lake," he said once his old friend rushed out.

"Sure. But I can't be gone too long."

Bundling up, they went outside and she breathed deeply, commenting, "Everything's so fresh today."

"That's what I love about this town. Every new day is exciting."

CC balked, and he asked "What?" in a half defensive, half good-natured way.

"Most people wouldn't say something like that about small town life," she offered.

"Having experienced big city life, I'm sticking to my assessment."

"I concur."

He nodded. "A lot has changed here in Sterling Lakes since my family moved out, and a lot has changed in my life in general. But coming back here has made me focus on the values that formed my character before I left. I think I needed the reminder of who I am, who I used to be, who I want to be. All the things I dealt with that caused me pain as an adult, made me build walls around myself..." He sighed as if having a hard time explain himself. "I don't know. Since I got here, I almost feel like I'm a lot shallower than I used to be, and I don't like that reflection of myself."

CC waited, feeling like something else was coming and not wanting to interrupt since he was confiding in her.

"I don't know what the future holds, but I think I'm ready to move on with my life, take back the best parts of my life before Diane died. My faith. My willingness to take a risk if that risk seems worth taking."

CC gulped out, "Like what?"

He drew in a deep breath. "Like... How about having dinner with me tonight?"

"A...date?"

He nodded, looking hopeful and a little fearful at the same time while holding her gaze.

She didn't leave him in misery long, but did manage to keep herself from pouncing on him in her eagerness. As coolly as her somersaulting inner being would allow her to, she said, "I'd love to go on a date with you, Perrin."

Happiness blossomed inside his chest as they continued walking in the crisp, cold down to the edge of the water. On the placid lakefront, loons and Canadian geese ignored them, too busy with their own pursuits to take any notice.

"So you and Cascade have known each other since you were kids?"

"Yeah."

"And you kept in touch all these years?"

Perrin glanced at her. "Honestly, no. We did a few jobs together, sporadically, in the last couple years. A few weeks before I came here, she called me, told me about the renovations at St Luke's. I said no right away. I'm embarrassed to admit it now, but I've been angry at God for years. Because he took Diane away from me just when we were both finally ready to start our lives together. I shouldn't have joined the military. I've thought that for years. It's really stupid for anyone to join the military and then get mad when there's a war and you have to do our duty. But I felt like I broke promises to Diane, made her wait--for our marriage to truly start, to have children together." His voice broke and he gasped, swallowed, tried to continue talking. "When I was finally discharged, we could have had the life we both dreamed of. But God took that away from me. That's what it felt like. So there was no way I was going to help rebuild the church."

Perrin tried to draw in another deep breath to calm him as they walked. Beside him, CC looked like she might burst out of her own skin, waiting, wanting to comfort him. He shook his head sheepishly at the memories. Unable to manage more than a whisper, he said, "About the time you start telling God no is when He starts making you rethink everything. I was chained to what happened and, until I got out of the past and moved into the new life He wanted me to have, there was no way I could function."

"So what did you do?" CC asked, sounding teary and her eyes were wet. Her compassion reached out to him like a tangible, living thing, wrapping him in balm.

"I went to my studio and smashed some stone. A lot of stone, all kinds. Some glass. And...after all that, I think I was the one that was shattered. I got down on my knees and prayed. I asked God what to do, asked Him to lead me, and I'd follow. Without question. There wasn't a doubt in my mind that I was supposed to come back to Sterling Lakes and help with the renovation. At that time, I never expected things to change the way they have..."

*Never expected to meet you. Feel something for another woman that's exciting and promising and potentially worth the pain I might someday feel if it doesn't work out.*

"So I called Cascade and told her I'd do it. And here I am."

CC heaved, wiping the tears from her cheeks, and he did the same with his own. "I'm really glad you did, Perrin." Her sweet smile was genuine, almost as good as a hug.

"So am I, CC. Have you been through times like that with God?" he asked, trying to compose himself.

She nodded. "Kind of. After Bobby dumped me, I went through something intense...less destructive."

He almost burst into tears at her welcome humor.

"But it made me realize I belonged to the Lord and, as long as He's with me, I'm who I should be. I'm *where* I should be. I'm doing what He wants me to. Everything's okay when He's the most important part of my life."

"That I understand. It required a lot of violence in my case, but sometimes we need to shatter and let God put us back together the way we should be."

Perrin reached for her hand and was pleased when she allowed him to take it. Squeezing gently, they looked out at the beautiful scene spread out before them, the sunlight glistening on the lake.

"I'm going to call a contractor today," CC said, sounding like she was putting on a brave front. "Cascade gave me a reference. I want to see what kind of work he thinks we can do on the attic. In the process, maybe we'll find your parents' love letters."

He turned in surprise. "I hope you're not going to pay for all that just to find the letters?"

"No, I told you I've wanted to do something with the attic since I first saw it."

"You also told me you were going to wait until you had the time and money."

Perrin turned to her, and she stopped in front of him. The cold had made her cheeks white but they were also rosy from the emotional overload. He couldn't help loving her sweet, innocent expression, even as he wondered if she planned to renovate her attic mainly so they could find those letters. "Are you sure you want to pay what probably won't be cheap to do something up in the attic?"

"Why wouldn't I?"

He swallowed, realizing that for the first time in so long he felt something so strongly for a woman, all he could think about was drawing her closer and kissing her. *And she wants me to. I can see that as obviously as if she painted the words across the sky.*

When his arms stole around her and they were close enough that their breaths mingled to become one white cloud, he murmured, "Meeting you has already changed my world, CC."

"Mine, too," she said in a whisper, but then she was closing the distance between them, her arms around his neck, and he couldn't remember a more perfect morning.

When she pulled back, they were both gasping a little and she groaned out loud. "I have to get going to work, or I'll be late. Could you please turn back the spin of the Earth, Superman? I'd like to never leave this moment."

Perrin smiled. "That makes two of us," he agreed before stealing another kiss that just might sustain him until he saw her again.

# Chapter 8

Russell Vigliani had already come and gone when CC got home late from work that evening--apparently without incident with her cat. She'd called the contractor on her drive to work that morning and told him the key was under the mat. Given that Cascade trusted the man, she had no trouble doing the same. He was going to check out the attic and see what he had to work with, given her ideas about putting in windows facing the lake so she could have a spot in the house to relax after work and just enjoy the scenery. She also mentioned she hoped to find some old letters in the attic that were presumably under the floorboards.

On the kitchen counter, beside his very reasonable estimate, was a huge stack of letters wrapped in a pretty ribbon. Russell wrote that he'd noticed one of the walls had a hollow sound to it and, without too much trouble, he'd found the hidden cubbyhole. The letters had been inside.

CC hadn't gotten a chance to even pick them up before her doorbell rang. She felt ragged from a long day of work and there wasn't time for the shower she'd intended before getting ready for her date with Perrin.

When she glanced out the sidelite window, she saw a huge Christmas tree that she could only assume someone was holding up. Even though she'd hoped to look beautiful beyond reason, her jumbled emotions made her not care. She was too filled with the memory of the kisses she'd shared with Perrin earlier today. *I'm fine, regardless of how disheveled.*

She pulled open the door eagerly. "Why, hello, Mr. Evergreen. I wasn't expecting a tree this evening."

Laughing, Perrin came around the tree, holding it with one hand while he used the other to ease her into a lingering kiss that thrilled her even as the fragrant tree wonderfully assailed her other senses. "Hello, Beauty. Surprise!" he said afterward, barely moving an inch from her. "A good one, I hope. I thought we could put up a Christmas tree together. Make some memories."

"That's a fantastic idea. Only I don't have any decorations."

"We'll worry about that later, another day. For now, let's get the tree up. I have the stand at least, if you don't mind carrying that in. We can go have dinner afterward."

Once he had the evergreen standing merrily in the living room, CC turned to see her cat looking at it with uncertainty, disdain, and finally snobbish dismissal. "Let's hope the old lady continues being uninterested in it after I get some shiny new ornaments to adorn it."

At dinner, Perrin told her that he'd gone to the Clarke's Falls quarry today and he'd worked out a deal with them that allowed a donation of a seriously discounted, beautiful piece of granite in a single block for the baptismal font while the business enjoyed a ton of publicity. In truth, he said, the fact that the owner of the quarry had known his dad had a lot to do with the generous donation.

"That's fantastic. How long do you think it'll take you to carve it?"

"Depends on a lot of things. But I'll have the piece next week and I can get started right away."

Though she gave him the encouragement he deserved, she couldn't help thinking that the sooner Perrin finished the font, the sooner he'd be leaving Sterling Lakes. *I don't like that thought at all.*

They ran into Patty and Elwood at the restaurant. When CC told them about her ornament-less tree, Patty said she had more than she could ever use at the B&B, though they were old-fashioned.

"You had me at 'I have a bunch I don't need anymore'," CC had stopped her in mid-protest.

Laughter felt almost giddy because she was with Perrin and life felt filled to bursting with potential.

"Then I'll have one of the girls set aside a few tubs of the old Christmas decorations for you, whenever you want to pick them up."

Getting into Perrin's rental, he drove them back to her cottage. "Hot chocolate?" she offered, hoping he wouldn't have to go already.

"You know I can never turn that down," he said with an eager grin.

Once inside, she realized she had to confess--even before they reached the kitchen. "Perrin, I have something to tell you. And it's not pleasant. I wish it was."

Surprising her because their romance was so new, he instantly took her in his arms, clearly wanting to comfort and be there for her.

*But I need to comfort and be there for him this time.*

"Look, why don't you go in the living room and make sure Bella didn't decide to knock down the tree? I have to grab something. I'll make the hot chocolate and bring everything in there when it's ready."

"Nothing's wrong, is there?" he asked in concern.

"It's about that journal, Perrin. I have good news and bad news. Try not to think about that too much before I get back, okay?"

He seemed astonished, a little distressed, but she knew she had to do this. After getting the hot chocolate on over a low burner, she went to get the original journal and her translation. As soon as their drinks were done, she put the mugs on a tray with the stack of letters and the journal pages covering them.

He was sitting on the sofa, staring at the Christmas tree. She could see the stress in his face when she handed him a mug, took one herself, then she sat next to him. He immediately moved in close so they were touching, facing each other.

"I'm not going to torture you, so the bad news first. Perrin, your father fell in love with another woman while he was stationed in Italy. That happened for the first seven months."

"What?"

"And your mother knew of this woman. Maria Bianco. She was a patient at the hospital your dad volunteered during his tour, and he spoke of her in his letters to her. Maria was mentally unstable, and your dad knew she was in love with him, wanted him to marry her, though he told her he was already engaged and couldn't break it because he loved his fiancée. Maria started calling him her husband. The long story short is, she died. She drowned. It's unclear whether it was an accident or not. Your dad always felt guilty about it. There's no way anyone could ever know whether she intended to drown herself that day or not. But he loved your mother, too, and he never had any intention of breaking their engagement because he made Helena promises first and he truly loved her."

Perrin was looking at her in a state of utter shock. "My mom talked about a Maria Bianco after Dad died, when I asked about his time in the service. All about Dad's volunteer work. About how Maria died so tragically. She said that really affected Dad. But Mom had no idea--"

"I don't know if your dad ever really wanted her to find out how deep his feelings went for Maria, Perrin. Even now. I think that's why he told you about his journal. Because he didn't want anyone to stumble on it and potentially have your mom and the three of you--his children--find out the truth that way. I think he wanted you to find them and make the decision about what to do with them."

Perrin shook his head, still disturbed. "What good news could there possibly be? You said you had good news and bad news."

She turned to set down her mug on the  coffee table, then picked up the loose pages. "In case you want to read the whole story, I translated his journal for you. And the contractor found your parents' love letters in a secret cubbyhole in the walls of the attic today while I was at work. I haven't looked at them or read them."

He took the beribboned stack, looking humbled and a little uncertain.

CC hugged him. "I know this can't be easy to hear, but I think your dad really loved your mom. Genuinely. Falling in love with Maria was just something that happened, a tragedy that he realized from the start wasn't right. But he was never inappropriate with her. He didn't betray your mother that way. And I think those letters your parents wrote to each other will show how much they loved each other all the time he was in Italy, despite what happened with Maria. Maybe your mom will find it in her heart to understand, if you show her all this. She might even forgive him. But what you do with all this is up to you. Your dad trusted you to make the decision."

Shell-shocked, Perrin muttered, "I wish he hadn't."

She nodded gently. "I know you want to understand all of this, though, and maybe... Listen, why don't you read his journal and some of the letters now? There's a lot of letters but I don't think you'll need to read them all. I'll run over to Patty's, grab those Christmas ornaments, and you can start reading while I decorate the tree. I'll make sure you have plenty of hot chocolate while we do."

"I...I don't want to ruin our date," he managed, but she could tell he wanted to do exactly what she suggested.

Pressing a kiss to his mouth, she assured him, "You won't. You can't. I want to be here after you read everything...in case you need someone."

He put down his mug and pulled her into a long, intense hug that put tears in her eyes. When he pulled away a scant inch, he kissed her. She lost her head so completely, she felt dizzy and delirious after, while he murmured, "You're the best thing that's happened to me in so long, CC. Thank you."

Perrin wasn't sure what he'd expected, especially after CC had given him the short version of the translated diary.

"Things make sense more," he said after he'd read the journal, including a good number of his parents' love letters--and they were that. Their deep, abiding love and desire for each other couldn't have come through clearer in the touching notes. His dad hadn't lied at all, though lies of omission might be considered hiding. Yet Perrin stopped reading, feeling his dad had done everything to prevent the situation from becoming sinful and, when he couldn't stop his feelings, he at least stayed true and honest to his morals and commitment to the Lord. He'd kept his honor, kept Maria's, and even kept his darling fiancée's in how he'd handled a situation that couldn't have been easy for him.

"When my dad told me about the journal and the letters, he said he'd spent his lifetime after his time in the service loving Mom, truly loving her, so she'd never doubt she was the woman he wanted to share his life with. I suppose he was thinking about Maria. He knew if I actually discovered the diary and letters, I'd find out the truth, and he wanted me to know that, too, so I could make sure Mom knew it if I decide to share all this with her."

CC sat down, taking a break from the half-decorated tree. "He seemed like a good man."

"He was. I've always believed it, and I worried when you told me he fell in love with another woman that my perceptions of him would change, but, if anything, I believe he was good stronger than ever now. Honestly, I don't know what I would have done in his place. Done *differently*."

"That letter Maria wrote to your dad, you mean, and he had the chaplain translate for him?" CC guessed.

He nodded. "Probably one of her last, truly lucid moments. It had to take a lot of guts to admit to a perfect stranger how terrified she was of the disease that was taking away the last vestiges of herself, who she was and the person she believed herself to be. And to have her own fiancé leave her like that... She was so lonely. Dad couldn't abandon her after she confided in him because she said life was too short to waste a minute. She needed someone to know who she was before it was too late. I can't help believing his love for her was pure--pure like God's love for us. He saw the beauty in her, and he didn't want her to be alone in the world."

"Maybe her drowning was just an accident. Or maybe she just didn't want her illness to consume her while she was alive so it seemed better to stop it from taking the last of her."

"That could be. It's so sad."

CC sighed, hugging him hard, just like he needed her to. "He loved her, and he loved your mom deeply. He was a hero who brought glory to those he knew, those he loved, to his country and his God."

Perrin sighed, agreeing. "My mom will be hurt at first when I tell her, but I think she'll be proud of Dad, too. She'll love him more."

"She learned life is short the hard way, too."

"Like I have. Yeah. I was stupid for wasting my life for so long, these past two years, but...grieving for someone I loved so deeply isn't a waste, is it? It's more like a memorial. A testimony to something precious that I'll never forget. But there is a time to move on, to start all over. And...I want that, CC. I want to move back to Sterling Lakes. There's nothing holding me in California. There's something I want right here, and I refuse to have any regrets. Life is too short not to live every moment and try to find happiness. So...what do you think?"

She gave a soft sigh. It didn't take much for Perrin to believe she was feeling like she was looking into the future, imagining a proposal that would be sweeter, more life-changing, but everything she ever wanted, just like he was.

"I can't think of anything I'd like more. Welcome home, Perrin."

Also available in the Sterling Lakes Series:
*Light of the Heart*, Book 1
*Angels of the Heart*, Book 2
*Praise of the Heart*, Book 3

If you enjoyed this author's book, then please place a review up at the site of purchase, and any social media sites you frequent!

**You can find ALL our books up on our website at:**

*https://www.writers-exchange.com*

**All Regina's Books:**

*https://www.writers-exchange.com/Regina-Andrews/*

**All our romances:**

*https://www.writers-exchange.com/category/genres/romance/*

# *About the Author*

A resident of Providence, R.I., Regina grew up in the nearby suburb of Barrington. After graduating from Providence College she attended the University of Delaware, and eventually returned to Providence to earn her Master's Degree in American Civilization from Brown University. She is inspired by the natural world and she and her husband enjoy visiting nearby Cape Cod, M.A. Some of her other hobbies include travel, museums, theater, classical music, coral singing, gardening, and anything French. In her spare time, she is a radio host for In-Sight Radio, a national association for the visually impaired of all ages.

For more on Regina's body of work, visit:

http://www.ReginaAndrews.com

For all of Regina's Writers Exchange books, go to her author page:

https://www.writers-exchange.com/Regina-Andrews/

**If you want to read more about other books by this author,**

**they are listed on the following pages...**

# Spotlight on Love

When duty calls, can love survive the battlefield?

Providence, 1941. Nurse Helen Middleton has sacrificed everything--her music, her youth, her dreams--to support her family during hard times. But when charismatic Postmaster William "Red" Williamson sweeps into her life with flowers, charm, and encouragement, Helen begins to imagine a future filled with song and love.

Then Pearl Harbor shatters the nation's innocence, and Helen's world turns upside down. Red is pulled into a dangerous covert mission overseas, while Helen enlists as an Army nurse and is deployed to war-torn North Africa. As espionage, betrayal, and tragedy close in, Helen must summon every ounce of courage to save the man she loves--and prove that even in the darkest times, love can light the way.

Fans of inspirational romance, wartime suspense, and strong heroines will be swept away by *Spotlight on Love*--a story of sacrifice, resilience, and the enduring power of the human heart.

Publisher: https://www.writers-exchange.com/spotlight-on-love/

# Sterling Lakes Series

{Inspirational Romance}

*Sterling Lakes is more than just a small New England town--it's a place where the past and present meet, where wounds run deep but faith runs deeper, and where God's light shines through the cracks of even the most broken hearts.*

*From a stained-glass artist haunted by childhood scars, to a journalist fighting to preserve history, a shy librarian learning to step into the light, and a war hero searching for hope after loss--the residents of Sterling Lakes discover that renewal begins within.*

*Each story in Regina Andrews' Sterling Lakes Series celebrates the courage to forgive, the beauty of second chances, and the glory of love that transforms lives. Against the backdrop of a town rediscovering its spirit, four romances intertwine to reveal a single truth: no matter the past, God's light can restore every heart.*

**LIGHT OF THE HEART**, Book 1: Cascade Preston swore she'd never return to Sterling Lakes.

The memories are too dark, the wounds too deep. But when a church renovation calls for her stained-glass artistry, Cascade finds herself face-to-face with both her past--and the determined project manager, Dan McQuay.

Dan refuses to take no for an answer. His steady presence and quiet faith begin to crack Cascade's protective shell. Yet opening her heart means risking the pain she's carried for years.

As the church rises from neglect, Cascade must decide: will she keep running from the town she associates with silence, or embrace forgiveness and the possibility of love?

Light of the Heart is a moving Inspirational Romance about second chances, healing from the past, and finding hope where you least expect it. Publisher: https://www.writers-exchange.com/light-of-the-heart/

**ANGELS OF THE HEART**, Book 2: Maryanne Lynch thrives on her career as a television journalist in Sterling Lakes. But nothing prepares her for the shock of developer Travis Collimore's plan to demolish the historic Townsend Barn--a landmark Maryanne treasures as part of the town's heart.

Determined to save the barn, Maryanne throws herself into the fight. But the more she opposes Travis, the more she glimpses the man beneath the title--a man whose quiet conviction stirs feelings she never expected.

With the town divided, Maryanne must decide if her heart belongs to the past she's protecting, or the future she might build with Travis.

Angels of the Heart is a heartfelt Inspirational Romance about trust, forgiveness, and love that can rise from even the fiercest of conflicts. Publisher: https://www.writers-exchange.com/angels-of-the-heart/

**PRAISE OF THE HEART,** Book 3: Laura Matthewson has always kept to herself. As Sterling Lakes' librarian, she finds comfort among books, not people--especially when all eyes are on the town's returning hero, baseball star Cliff Markham.

Cliff came home to help raise funds for St. Luke's Church, but he didn't expect to be drawn to the shy librarian who avoids the spotlight. Laura's gentle spirit captivates him, yet she struggles to believe she belongs in his world.

As the fundraiser heats up, Laura must face her fears and decide whether to keep hiding in the shadows--or step into the light of love and faith.

Praise of the Heart is a tender Inspirational Romance about courage, community, and discovering the strength God placed within you.
Publisher: https://www.writers-exchange.com/praise-of-the-heart/

**GLORY OF THE HEART**, Book 4: CC Cogshell came to Sterling Lakes for a fresh start. A former detective with a broken heart, she's determined to rebuild her life on her own terms. The last thing she expects is Perrin Stafford--a decorated war hero and sculptor--showing up on her doorstep just before Christmas.

For Perrin, returning to his childhood home stirs bittersweet memories. Grieving his late wife and burdened by secrets from his father's past, he's unsure whether faith--or love--has a place in his future.

Drawn together by chance, CC and Perrin discover that healing sometimes comes in unexpected ways. Between attic discoveries, holiday traditions, and the glow of a church reborn, they must decide if they're willing to let go of the past and embrace the glory God offers in the present.

Glory of the Heart is a moving Inspirational Romance about second chances, faith restored, and love that shines brightest in the darkest seasons.
Publisher: https://www.writers-exchange.com/glory-of-the-heart/

# The Perfect Proposal

Lindsay Richardson never expected her new job at Copley Industries to change her life. One chance interview with the elder Mr. Copley lands her a position she desperately needs—but also puts her face-to-face with his son, Dean Singleton Copley, the commanding executive who allows no room for mistakes.

To Dean, business comes first, last, and always. But Lindsay's resilience and warmth prove difficult to ignore. As deadlines mount and Boston glitters with Christmas lights, she challenges Dean to see beyond contracts and control.

Between family traditions, church gatherings, and the quiet hope of the season, love begins to grow in unexpected places.

Can the holidays soften Dean's guarded heart, or will fear and pride keep him from making the perfect proposal?

A warm and wholesome holiday romance, *The Perfect Proposal* is perfect for readers who love Christmas settings, clean romance, and happily-ever-afters.

Publisher: https://www.writers-exchange.com/the-perfect-proposal/

# *If you want to read more about other Romance novels by this publisher, they are listed on...*

https://www.writers-exchange.com/category/genres/romance/

## You can find ALL our books up on our website at:

https://www.writers-exchange.com

## All Regina's Books:

https://www.writers-exchange.com/Regina-Andrews/